Praise for *This Is My*

'A spectral succession of [...]
that one cannot help but [...]
hearts imbued in each. I was allured and delighted in equal
measures.'

— **Matt Wesolowski, author of the *Six Stories* series**

'Heather Parry is one of my favourite writers. These stories are
strange, bold, queer and surprising — all my favourite things.
A stunning debut collection.'

— **Kirsty Logan, author of**
Now She Is Witch* and *Things We Say in the Dark

'A remarkable collection that shines a harsh light on the dark
underbelly of humans and humanity, with an occasional flash
of slyly absurd humour. Shocking, visceral, intimate and honest,
and genuinely disturbing and outrageous in its horrific detail.
There's a dark mind at work here.'

— **Lucie McKnight Hardy, author of**
Dead Relatives* and *Water Shall Refuse Them

'No one knows how to twist the body quite like Heather Parry.
Through mistaken menses stigmata, to sentient sex dolls who
collect the muttered moans of male clients, the stories in *This
Is My Body, Given For You* breach the boundaries of the skin
with sparkling prose. In some circles of fiction it's taught that
the body is the place where all stories begin — Parry brings this
home in the most macabre and dazzling way.'

— **Elle Nash, author of *Animals Eat Each Other***

Praise for *Orpheus Builds A Girl*

'A compelling, creepy tale – and one that raises relevant questions about who 'owns' a woman's body.'

– The Independent

'Superbly creepy from the start… It's a modern take on classic Gothic fiction, and while it certainly owes a debt to the likes of Mary Shelley's *Frankenstein*, it breaks new ground of its own and will chill readers to the bone. Disturbing and compelling in equal measure.'

– The Big Issue

'A chilling story of deranged infatuation, medical abuse, coercion and power.'

– The Skinny

'A wild, creepy, compelling read.'

– Jan Carson

'A deliciously macabre voyage through one man's grotesque lunacy and the destruction he leaves in his wake. Parry skilfully evokes the horror at the heart of the tale, painting a series of hallucinatory images as the narrative reaches an extraordinary finale, where the organic is pushed into monstrous proportions.'

– Martin MacInnes, author of Infinite Ground

Published by Haunt Publishing
www.hauntpublishing.com
@HauntPublishing

ISBN (paperback): 978-1-915691-04-0
ISBN (ebook): 978-1-915691-05-7

Cover design by Esther Clayton: extrateeth.co.uk

Typeset by Laura Jones: lauraflojo.com

Printed and bound in Great Britain by Clays Ltd, Elcograf S.p.A

Printed with the support of Lighthouse Bookshop, Edinburgh

This Is My Body, Given For You

To Ada
Thanks for coming to
Category Is!

HEATHER PARRY

♡

HAUNT
PUBLISHING

in memory of Jasper Hamlet
(1990–2020)

and for Jennie

The body is not a thing, it is a situation.

— SIMONE DE BEAUVOIR, *THE SECOND SEX*

Contents

Content notes: abuse; body horror; death; gore; grief; kidnapping; miscarriage; rape; sexism; sexual abuse and assault.

first: a shocking (but morally unchallenging) story, to pique the reader's interest

AMELIA MAGDALENE

It was a blessing when my blood came. At school they said it would be spots and strings, but to my surprise it was a steady stream, dark red, pouring out from the corners of my eyes and puddling on the tops of my battered brogues. I held back a retch and when the urge to faint passed, I shouted for Daddy, excited, from the top of the stairs. Squinting into the light from the landing, he said *God bless us, Joyce, it's a miracle.* My mother, hunched over like she'd been screwed up and thrown away, strained to look up at me and screamed. As she fled back to her overcooked potatoes, Daddy took the crusty hanky from his back pocket and wiped the blood across my nose and cheeks, making more of a mess than there was before. He shoved the hanky into my hand. Grinning, grateful, I pocketed the soaked cotton. As Daddy strode into the kitchen, I heard his voice rise:

Hospital? She needs an agent, not a hospital.

There were to be no doctors. Daddy's word was always final, not because he was the stronger of the two, but the weaker. Despite never finding work, he ruled with a ceaseless sense of self-importance that nobody could bear to wrench from him; my mother, with her twisted spine, carried the

two of us on her uncomplaining back. My first thought
when I looked into the mirror and saw two trickles of scarlet
running from my eyes had been *Daddy is going to love this.*

That night, he watched me over dinner, wads of old tea
towels taped to my cheeks so the blood wouldn't drip onto
my eggs. My mother fretted over the creeping red cracks in
the whites of my eyes, but Daddy just stared. Sometimes he
smiled, and sometimes I smiled back.

The office of Oswald Merman was white and gold, a dressing room for potential starlets; a mock Versailles. All platinum
blonde and crisp white cotton with a shock of electric blue
beneath his lapels, Merman tentatively reached over to his
phone, side-eying me like I was a glass of red wine waiting
to tip. Daddy patted my arm again – to relax himself rather
than me, I knew – and nodded to no one in particular, his
greying head bobbing as if he was a plastic dog on the back
shelf of someone's car. A silicone baby's bib, complete with a
crumb-catcher that had to be emptied every couple of hours,
hung from my ears and fit tightly around my chin.

*Cynthia, could you get the Vatican on the phone? I've no idea;
you'll have to look in the yellow book.*

They were saying things like *percentage cut* and *security detail*
and *power of attorney.* I squinted at the portrait over Merman's
shoulder to see if it was of a man or a woman. Everything was
opaque and lacked edges. My hands twitched, itching to wipe
and scratch at my sore sockets, but I knew Daddy needed me
not to. I buried my fingers beneath my bottom. My eyelids
worked overtime but still couldn't wipe my vision clean, so I
closed them, letting the sound of Merman's words distract me.

Oh. It seems to have… Mr Parsons?

The raw liver dissolved on my tongue and Daddy nodded encouragingly, pretending that neither of us could hear my mother vomiting into the kitchen bin. Liver for lunch, kidneys for dinner, black pudding for breakfast; it was my new regime, intended to bring back the blood tears that had dried up, seemingly of their own accord, right before Daddy signed my name on Merman's dotted line. Daddy thought it was a lack of iron, or plasma, or something or other that he'd read in the mouldy medical books now stacked in the bathroom. Mother told him it was just one of those things. Each morning he checked my sheets for stains, running into my room when he heard me close the bathroom door, then scuttling dejectedly down the stairs to my mother as he heard me flush.

Three weeks later, Daddy had cultivated quite the relationship with the local butcher, who loved his spike in profits, but my eyes were still dry, the skin around them recovering slowly. The details of my world were starting to come back into focus and it seemed like everything was returning to normal, the episode a single occurrence destined to be remembered in parentheses. Daddy's panicked positivity, however, could not be quelled. On the Monday, he announced that my diet was doubling. On the Thursday, I woke with a thin bolt of pain running across my torso and spent the day in bed, tended to by my limping mother, while Daddy fed me liver smoothies and kidney soup and examined the veins in my arms when he thought I wasn't looking.

On the Saturday, the red tears came once again, this time with errant stringy lumps that I had to pull past my tear ducts and away from the path to my mouth.

It's her monthlies, said my mother. *By God, it's her curse.*

Daddy got me a bruised Bible from the local charity shop and an off-white dress that touched the tops of my toes. To watch him working, creating, brought a warmth to my face; he'd always been an inventor on the side. When I was two, it was a stuffed toy with a heat-pad stomach and a clock inside that burned my thigh and gave me tinnitus. Just after I'd started school, it was an electrical washing-up device with robot arms that fell into the sink and caused a kitchen fire. When I was five, my mother lost her eyebrows in a complicated incident involving a mechanical set-up that pulled the sheets back every morning. But he needed the hope, the belief that someday his name would be attached to something great, so we kept our mouths shut when he sunk more of our savings into his projects and invalidated the house insurance time and time again.

But Daddy, I told him, *I can't see the words,* as he showed me the passages he'd underlined during a sleepless night of planning. He read the verses to me as he fed me orange juice and Pop-Tarts, a sweet treat after so much offal, and I got so good at repeating them back between sugary mouthfuls that neither of us heard my mother's frantic yelps until she'd been calling for thirty minutes. With no one to help her reach the wall-mounted rail that allowed her to get out of bed, she'd stretched too far and fallen, her cheek grazing the unvarnished wood of my parents' bedroom floor. We hauled her up to her feet but her spine, robbed of its morning exercise, had locked itself into an angry question mark, an exaggeration of her normal condition. I wrapped my legs around her and massaged the spaces between her vertebrae. Daddy said that once we'd made it to our meeting, she could take the car and drive herself to the hospital.

Merman had told the others waiting in his antecham-
ber — six-fingered boys, overgrown teens, women with
well-groomed facial hair — that he wasn't taking any more
appointments. They trudged out mournfully as the three of
us followed Cynthia, who seated us briskly then dispensed
sugary black coffees that we had not ordered and did not
want. Merman asked Daddy question after question. My
mother, unwilling to leave me, held my hand; her eyes closed,
her palm spasming in pain from time to time. Cynthia,
disgusted with the job now taking her away from diarising
and coffee-making, swabbed the sore flesh under my eyes
and apologised curtly before sealing the cotton in a test tube
and noting the date on the label. I stood up and she patted
me down, running her hands between my aching breasts and
up my back to feel for plastic lines or other trickery. She
patted my shoulder and nodded. Seeing that we were done,
my mother uncurled herself and slipped her arm around my
waist, unburdening some of her weight, as she led me out to
our Volvo.

Apologies, Angelo, I heard Merman say to Daddy as my
mother and I left the office. *I've got to be sure; too many court
cases these days, you know. Now, let's talk scheduling.*

Before I could say anything to the hospital receptionist, my
mother reached across the desk, grabbed both of the woman's
grey hands and said *Please, you've got to help my daughter.* There
were gasps as the strangers on the plastic chairs forgot their
personal maladies and turned around to look at me. The
receptionist, shaken, led us straight through to an examination

room. My mother talked over me every time I tried to insist that we were there on her account, for the agony in her back. One doctor came, then two, then other fuzzy figures in white coats and blue scrubs filled up the less distinct corners of the room. My virginity was taken on crunchy hospital paper by a smooth piece of cold metal, with a mass of medical staff staring between my spread legs and my mother holding my hand. The hysteroscope projected a moving image onto the plasma screen by my head, but all I could see was a mass of flesh that looked like it was crawling. I stared at the ceiling until the cold thing slid out of me, unsure whether to feel ashamed, embarrassed or proud.

Well, it's just the strangest thing. She's wired perfectly, Mrs Parsons. The lining's all there. It's just not coming out where it's meant to.

My mother asked if I'd have babies still, and though the doctor said that he couldn't see why not, someone right by my head huffed and said, *I think someone's got other plans for that girl.*

They prescribed me drops for my stinging eyeballs and arranged an appointment with specialists from the mainland. A week later when the letter dropped on the mat, Daddy barely glanced at the headed paper before he tore it into pieces and said, through gritted teeth, *But Darling, you're going to be famous!*

After that, there was no time for school. With just twenty-one days until my inaugural performance and only seven potential show days per month, it was rehearsals from the moment my tears dried to the moment they came again. I started to think of time only in cycles of twenty-eight days. Merman closed his offices and came over every morning, calling me things like *Our Starlet* and touching the ends of my hair. My mother stayed in the kitchen while I recited verses in the glow of a makeshift spotlight, but she made me a cucumber eye mask to soothe my aching sockets and defied Daddy's carnivorous diet plan to feed me cold carrot juice every night. Daddy and Merman broke the lock on my diary to check the dates of my cycle and draw up a schedule, and on day twenty-seven of that month I was christened and reborn; the name in neon lights was *Amelia Magdalene*.

All press is good press, trilled Merman as he paced excitedly around me, fanning himself with a national newspaper that, they told me, had my school photo on the front. He and Daddy were too busy planning PR responses to tell me what it said, but my mother had taken a break from our rehearsals to read the whole thing out loud. A reporter had paid our next-door neighbour a grand to steal the liver-smeared blender from our kitchen, and the resulting article was a blizzard of insult and conjecture, calling me a fraud and Daddy a liar.

We'll put up the ticket prices by half, said Merman. *You're a bona fide star now, girl.* He grabbed me by the shoulder, then grimaced as he wiped my mess from his forearm. I could still catch the shimmer of him in the dim light of the dressing room as he swam around in the near dark, a siren for those seeking salvation. He and Daddy disappeared into a shadowy corner and said things like *defamation* and *libel* and *great publicity*. I closed my sore eyelids and let the words of the Lord, recited by my mother, drown out the cold phrases of business.

It turned out that Merman was right. We moved to larger venues, auditoriums that had no ceilings and theatres so old that they had no lifts. My mother had to drag herself up spiral staircases behind my growing entourage. After I'd been on the evening news, Daddy bought me designer glasses with the name of a footballer's wife on the side. They shielded me from the lightning bolts of cameras and, as Daddy put it, *protected our best assets*. With every show, details dropped away and my depth perception suffered. My mother taught me to see by feel, running my hands over the dressing tables and plush sofas in every new city, keeping my fingers away from my face lest I ruin the perfect streams.

We touched down in France on a Tuesday. The flights had been booked so that I'd already be bleeding, ready for the press on the runway, but we arrived late after a delay of six panicked hours when the miracle had declined to begin at its scheduled time. I could see too much; the light was more than I had glimpsed in months. I clutched my boarding pass and willed the tears to come. Daddy prayed and Merman barked at anonymous assistants, ordering them to bring ten feet of plastic tubing and an IV bag. Airport authorities fussed and snarled in the doorway of the first-class lounge and were shooed away by my mother. I lay down with my head in Daddy's lap and dozed off while Merman measured my torso. When I finally blinked awake, the world was shadowed once more and a cheer went up in the room. Three hours later we landed in Lourdes, the heat of the air making my tears drip faster as my mother described the thousands waiting on the airstrip. Their weeping hymns brought up the goosebumps on my arms and made me hold Daddy's hand a little tighter.

There were three performances a day, each one attended by two hundred more than could really fit into the Church of Our Lady, or so I was told, and though the verses had been burned into memory by my mother's ceaseless repetition, I found that my role was much smaller than I'd imagined. I stood in my darkness, arms slightly turned away from my body, and I let them all watch while my uterus lining ran down my face in thick furrows and the priest's words echoed around me. I spoke only when prompted, a few lines about forgiveness, and held my palms out to be kissed by the mouths of a thousand faceless strangers when the Father pushed me to my knees at the edge of the stage.

We upped the schedule to six shows a day, my eyes settling into a quiet but constant pain that coated the inside of my skull. I touched my fingertip to my cheek and licked the wetness there to know if the show could still go on; it stopped tasting metallic on day eight, though Daddy said we'd been blessed with one more day than normal because we were doing God's will.

That final day in Lourdes was one long performance. The Father took my hands and placed them on the bodies of those with unworking limbs and skin ravaged by disease, their pustules and bedsores oozing beneath my fingertips while they told me of weeklong journeys from Israel, Australia, Ireland and beyond. *Twelve thousand*, someone said, as silhouettes came and went before my outstretched palms. Daddy brought me ice-cream and juice, the sweetness punctuating seven sour days of steak tartare and the body of Christ, and as I felt the warmth of the sun burn through stained glass windows, I prayed to keep feeling the glow of Daddy's happiness.

Seven weeks later, I realised we weren't going home.

I never saw Italy. The tyres touched the tarmac on day twenty-eight of my ninth cycle, to give us time to settle in before the main event and recover from the righteous insanity of Guatemala. Daddy gripped me, quivering with joy at having finally become somebody, the father of a miracle child, as he described the hordes of believers raising their hands from their eyelids to the skies in worship, thanking the Lord himself for his blessing. Not a word reached my ears, though, as I was lifted by thick biceps into a vehicle – an armoured limo, Merman said – and handed a glass of something fizzy that tingled up my nose. My mother pressed my hands against the walls of the hotel, which were patterned with velvet, and she told me that within the grand suite there were rooms enough for one each, though Daddy slept atop my covers, waking hourly to check with the large men at my doorway. The next morning, I woke on my back with my arms straight out from my shoulders and still didn't touch the sides of the mattress, adrift in an endless sea of decadence. The light had all gone from the world, though, even the shadows, even the shapes. My eyes were weeping, but it tasted yellow, of pus, and my mother coughed out an embittered cry when I staggered, unseeing, from my haven.

There must have been a number of different doctors, all speaking in tongues, none saying a word to me. Merman yelled at translators at the foot of my bed as gloved fingers dabbed and touched and bathed and anointed me. The weathered skin of my mother's hands, the skin of a hard life, rested on my forehead. I listened to the constant low moan that had replaced her voice.

Just make it stop, will you? snapped Merman. *Not antibiotics, we need something that will work right now!*

Arguments broke out and I clutched my mother's thigh, willing myself into sleep so I didn't have to hear. I woke to the rustle of sheets that smelled clinical, the clatter of metal instruments and the aggressive heat of lamps not far from my face. With a little pressure and a nick on my inner arm, they told me to count back from ten, and by four I had fallen into a woolly unconsciousness. When I came around, there were tight, stinging lines under my eyes, the flesh throbbing. Someone applied a drizzle of liquid that burned right through to my ear. A heavily accented voice spoke just before tablets were put in my mouth and my throat was rubbed to make me swallow as if I were a recalcitrant cat.

The drainage was successful, but the infection might still come back. She'll need the medication for at least ten days, but I urge you to cancel the meeting. That girl needs a hospital, not a blessing.

11

The next morning, the metallic taste dripped into my mouth and my tear ducts ached. I pulled gently and removed thick clumps of menstrual blood from just below my eyeballs, my face still puffy and painful, my mind still cloudy and warm. My body and head were covered in a coarse material, the thick cotton cutting around my neck. Sharp fingernails applied thick-scented lotions and powders to my face as Daddy and Merman spoke to the press outside the door, and I giggled a painkiller giggle, tickled by the way the brushes caught on my eyelashes. In the early afternoon, a man called from beyond the door and my mother kissed my forehead, halting as if she was going to say something before scurrying away from my bed. A swarm entered the room, the voices all male, and hands carried me out to a car. I couldn't quite grasp onto anything, couldn't quite shake away the fuzziness in my head, and I wondered if it really was Daddy weeping next to me, kissing my hands and calling me an angel. When the car pulled to a halt, delicate fingers dabbed the clotted blood out of my painted eyes and led me out into the harsh sun.

Our steps echoed off marble walls as we entered the building, the searing heat giving way to astonishing cold. I let myself be taken, hushed voices whispering *Holy Father* and *Your Grace*, and when I was put onto my knees, I kissed the warm metal on the fingers in front of my mouth, as I had been told to do.

She'll be a saint, said a bodiless voice, and I thought, *Daddy must be so proud*.

second: rebirths

    wherein the writer, having previously offended or upset the reader, offers stories that may instil a sense of hope, or perhaps a comforting confusion, from which may arise a willingness to consider an alternative view of things, or if not that, the creation of a web of surreality, a rejection of the material, from which the reader cannot escape

THE
BASTARD-OCTOPUS

after Roland Barthes

T he limbs of the costumed cephalopod wrap around his opponent and tighten, rendering the man inert. The crowd give heat; as one, they jeer and boo, a disguised adoration. They live for this. They spit their pantomime displeasure onto the skin of others. They breathe in the foetid stench of the fighters, see the tears of sweat drip from one man to the other. They suckle at soda teats and scream themselves hoarse at the injustice they expect and demand. In the ring, the trapped man is scooped, three arms between his legs and three around his neck, lifted like he is weightless, held for a moment then slammed down onto the canvas. The impact of the body disperses droplets of blood from a puddle in the wet ring. The blood of other wrestlers, of fights before theirs. The crowd reacts with manic outrage. It is sweeter than usual.

The stunned body rises. Steadies itself. The Bastard-Octopus resists, holding back from the easy attack. This is his role, but he does not want it. Cheers. Goading. Parts of him respond to the coaxing. His dexterous arms swim as if casting a spell. They linger in the air. He stands as he appears on his poster, chest high, face gurning anger, arms lifted: *six arms, two legs, one hell of an attitude! The most repugnant bastard there is: The Bastard-Octopus!* As if called, his many arms grab. They wrap. The other fighter's hands respond, the two lock up, but six arms overpower two. The crowd surges forward to look for mechanics, electronics, engineering. They marvel at the smooth movement of the antagonist, the way his arms seem part of him. The Bastard-Octopus fills himself up, draws all power into his chest, pauses, drives his opponent into the turnbuckle. The thrown man sags and slips to the canvas. There is no movement. The crowd ignites. The fight is over quickly, too quickly for the money they have paid, but they don't mind. They come for the righteous indignation. They leave satisfied.

The Bastard-Octopus retires to his dressing room. The other fighters bathe in the women and booze that come to them. They gather sweaty and imbibe intoxicants, their manufactured gripes left in the ring. The Bastard-Octopus does not join them. He rushes to his solitude. Behind the closed door, he slips his two legs and six arms out of his outfit, an outfit that has been cleverly created to give four of his upper limbs the illusion of fakeness. He slides into the shower, employing numerous bars of soap and all his appendages to the mammoth task of freshening his armpits, then towels off with impressive speed. He stands at the mirror, looking for injuries. None.

He takes his lowest arm and presses bicep to torso. He bends it at the elbow, wrapping it around his stomach. He does the same with his next arm, which sits on top of the first. The two lowest arms on each side form a protective shell around his upper body, then he takes an elastic bandage and wraps. The arm shell tightens. The bandage constricts. He adds an inch or so of girth, but not more. Swaddled in himself, only two arms free, he struggles into a shirt and then a hoodie, despite the fact that he will sweat through both. He looks passably normal. He turns the light of the hallway off before he strides down it, head bowed, trying not to catch the attention of the fighters at the bar as he makes for his vehicle. Someone shouts something, but he's learned not to hear.

The Bastard-Octopus spends nights at his local gym. In the absence of other customers, he whiles away the hours until sunrise training. He squats, letting his favoured arms hold the bar and willing the rest to stay by his side. But the arms still reach up, still try to ease the burden of the weight. They are part of him, but he cannot control them. He attempts to train not his upper arms, not his legs, not even his glutes – but the arms that move despite him. He lifts and carries and pushes, but it is the unwanted appendages that he concentrates on, willing them to stay down, to lose function, to flop around gracelessly. But they do not. They press their palms to the floor and lift his body. They grab the tyre, the kettlebell, the pull-up bar. They act, and he cannot stop them. Exhausted, as the day breaks, he heads home – to sleep, to hide, to wait for the night.

As his next match nears, he calls a number that has been given to him online, in forums, where he uses a fake female name and complains of aging. The voice at the end of the line expresses concern about the amounts requested, triples the agreed-upon fee and tells him where to pick up a package. In a darkened garage, under the cover of night, The Bastard-Octopus stuffs the contraband into his bandages and races back to his car.

He cannot afford to waste any of the material on testing. He stands in front of his mirror as at the end of the corridor, the crowd screech and boo at the wrestlers already engaged in the ring. He stands naked, costume-free, and cracks the first syringe out of its housing. He takes the cold point and traces it along the bicep of his lowest arm. He pauses a moment then slams the needle into the muscle. A straight pain. He expends it, empties the barrel. Feels a breeze rush into the tiny hole left by the needle. He tosses the used syringe into an old toolbox he's brought for the purpose, and starts the process over again, this time with the forearm. He waits. Heat envelops the arm, spreading out from the shoulder to the tips of his nails. The muscles shake, fight against the toxin. Perspiration covers his skin. The arm becomes leaden, drops. Overtaken by a flaccid paralysis. Beaming, The Bastard-Octopus punches the arm with a spare fist. It hangs, limp, useless. He could weep. He takes the remaining syringes and goes through it all again; eight syringes, in total, for four arms. Bundling the lifeless appendages clumsily into the arms of his costume, he turns his body from side to side like a child.

Four of his arms flop, slap, knock things over. Outside the door, his name is called. Ecstatic, he runs to the ring, heavy and cumbersome, lolling like a weighted ship. He drags his mass into the humid ring and surrenders.

The Bastard-Octopus never reads the script, for his body never follows the script. When the fighter comes for him, he is loose and unprepared. He is punched. He is lifted, arms encircling his torso, his eyes closed. His upper back slams to the ground as he is suplexed first once, then twice, then a third time. The pain of it is sweet, narcotic; he looks to his arms, prostrate on the canvas, twitching in agony. The crowd murmurs, unsure. This is unwritten, to their minds. The heel has turned victim. His opponent grabs his hand, lifts one of his active arms, and wraps his thick legs around it. He laces his fingers around The Bastard-Octopus's wrist, his crotch against the covered skin, lets himself fall back onto the canvas, and wrenches the arm from its socket. For a moment, The Bastard-Octopus feels his arm removed from his body, tendons ripped, chest muscle separated from ligament. His heart seizes; the loss of it stuns him. He feels impotent. Six down to one. What has he done? The crowd is quiet, near silent. He is hauled to his feet, steadied, set up for another attack. He clutches his one strong arm to the one numb and detached; he feels the rest of them stir, want to help, want to reach up and assist. The torn arm twitches. He breathes. It is still stitched to his body. He pushes all his effort into movement; it shifts. It remains. It tingles, but so do the others. He is still whole. He grimaces, a true reaction, but not for the reasons the audience assume. The other fighter is gleeful, intending to hurt. He steps back, giving distance, creating a show. He plays to the audience, receives little response, and grows angrier. The Bastard-Octopus closes his eyes as the man runs at him, readying his bent body for a running drop kick aimed right at the head.

The crowd detonates. Screeching cheers that burn the ears. He opens his eyes; the other fighter has been flung past him, over the ropes, over the guard rail, into the braying crowd. Red-faced and raging, the man climbs back into the ring, mounts the turnbuckle, prepares himself for a vengeful pounce. He jumps. Flies. The Bastard-Octopus watches as his four heavy arms, rendered obsolete just moments ago, raise themselves up and catch the man, wrapping him, chest to chest, lifting him and slamming him onto the canvas with an aggression that pains them both. From there, he cannot watch. Inside him, a rock falls down an endless well. His eyes are open, but he does not see the rest. He does not need to. It has all been written, and the crowd are delighted.

Five wins in a row. Seven. Twelve. The crowds grow and grow, but the promoters aren't happy. They tell him to hang back, to stand off, to let the others get a few moves in, a few wins. But he cannot. With incredible will, he can hold off his own body for a short while, but eventually it takes over. Mere minutes of restraint, just a little fair contest, then he reaches out, embraces his opponent, crushes the body to his chest, overwhelms him. The crowds keep coming, and so he keeps being booked, but the other fighters pour drinks on him as he leaves the ring, leave shit in his gear bag, hammer nails into his tyres. They, too, think that the arms are mere costuming: a gimmick, a trick of the senses. They think him a cheat, and a freak one at that.

At the mirror, The Bastard–Octopus flexes, spreads out like a peacock. His hated arms are growing, filling out, taking up more space. The effort of throwing and crushing huge bodies stimulates them. More bandage is needed to wrap them against him, and the resulting bulk is harder to hide. In the day, he cannot sleep, for no matter where he turns, there's a limb beneath him. On his few necessary trips into the society of others, he looks gross, a lumpen creature, knocking pensioners and children out of the way; he doesn't even see them. *The most repugnant bastard there is.*

Twenty wins in a row and the fight time down to seconds. They have to book his fights at the end of others, to avoid real displeasure from the spluttering, screeching crowd who now pay double. He is a destroyer, and the other fighters come away with broken bones and loose teeth. They place increasing demands on the promoters for his removal, but the promoters see the money streaming in and act only to placate. After each match, the uninjured fighters wait for him in the car park. Set at him with iron bars and base-ball bats – but always beneath the neck, always at the torso, keeping his resulting injuries from being so easily seen. One beating is so brutal that when he unbinds his torso and his hidden arms fall free, one lies limp and desolate and remains that way for days. The Bastard-Octopus, buoyed, feels a hope grow within him.

He loads the bar with another weight. There are only two left on the floor. Sitting beneath the apparatus, he takes deep breaths. He has pre-emptively consumed codeine, whisky, weed, but he knows it will still hurt. The fuzziness will be sliced through like soft cheese, but there is nothing left to do. He meditates as much as he can, lays his two lowest arms on the floor, where he has marked lines with chalk. His arms are at a strange angle and cannot lie flat, but he supposes this will help the results. With his uppermost hands, he rolls the bar along the platform he has created. He teases it along with his fingers, towards the edge, and in a moment it drops. The white filter of trauma engulfs him; his ears buzzing, his tongue fat and dry, his mouth screaming miles from his ears. When he stops writhing, he looks to the bar, which has rolled off his arms, over to the edge of the room and cracked the bottom of the mirror. His two arms are snapped, covered in blood, skewered by smashed bone. Euphoria overcomes him. Energised by frantic shock, he takes himself to his car, drives home, collapses into bed. When he wakes, his breaks are healed, the agony remaining, but his ruined arms still move, still act, still dance in time with the rest of them. In a matter of days, they function fully. The promoter calls, booking the biggest fight of his life. He prepares with a listless horror. It has been written.

The Bastard-Octopus stands, his hand raised by the referee, the sell-out crowd hawking and screeching, snarling and snapping, pushing the heads of others out of their view. Beside him, the rising star of the wrestling world, the new face of the company. The Bastard-Octopus is under strict instruction to look up at the lights, to lay down and take his loss with little damage to his opponent. He hears a whispered reminder, but brushes it away. He is a man committed. There is no going back.

The all-star swings at him with a lariat, his arm solid, unyielding. The Bastard-Octopus flips backwards, crashes to canvas, heavy. The tension within him is gone. He is in no hurry. His arms stay prone, ready. A physical patience. He is thrown and pummelled, canvas at his back, at his front, against his teeth. Serenity overtakes him. A quiet in his mind. This is no work, no dance of pretended violence. The reality of the hurt is meditative. The time comes. A brief respite from his opponent. He rises up. He lifts all six of his arms, each one engaged, each one accepted, and envelops the man running towards him. Stopped, the man yelps. Six biceps strain to keep him in place, distended veins mapping his skin, sweat pouring. Six hands fasten themselves around the limbs, around the torso, around the neck. Six arms lift the body, almost throw him upwards, pause, then in one explosive motion, smash him mercilessly into the ground. The canvas gives, bounces back, sends the ruined spine briefly upwards again. Then it settles, the carcass at the wrestler's feet, and the audience, words caught in their throats, scream a dense silence. The only sound: a withered groaning from the broken man, an involuntary noise from collapsed lungs, a rattle. Six fists dig nails into palms, six trails of blood drip slowly. The Bastard-Octopus takes in the derision, the hatred, the spite. Real. Alone amongst the frozen tableau, he lifts the ropes and leaves the ring. No one comes to stop him.

He showers. Towels down. Does not wrap his arms, nor cover himself with clothes, but leaves his dressing room bare-chested, with his chin held high. Backstage there is no one, no drinkers at the bar.

He knows it is coming. He steps out into the night and fixes his eyes on the metal. He ducks, unconsciously, so the iron bar hits his forehead, not his nose as intended. After that, a soft nothing.

He wakes in his bed. He is glad that he is not in hospital, with their gross testing and inevitable labels. Around his bed there is medical equipment. Bunches of flowers, boxes of chocolates, cards saying *Get Well Soon*. The promoters have paid for this; he knows, then, that it was another fighter that did the damage. This is hush-hush care. That he is still so valuable to them means he has not been shopped to a hospital, to the press, to a medical researcher. But still, he is alone, cared for by electronics. He is comforted by this. By his bed there is a printed sheet:

Please do not attempt to move. You have suffered a spinal injury. You are strapped to a brace. Someone will check on you in the morning and will help you if you are awake.

Outside, the sun is almost hidden. The Bastard-Octopus closes his eyes, and for the first time in his adult life, sleeps in the darkness.

The nurse comes three times a day. She explains to him that along with his fractures and breaks, he has damaged his spinal cord, making his prognosis difficult. One day, with wriggling toes, he is allowed free of his brace and sits up, slightly unsteady but confident. He shakes his legs, turns his head, coughs. The nurse is stunned. He goes to push himself up off the bed, but something is wrong. His hands – he does not know where they are. The sense of feeling their space in the world, their location, their actions – it is missing. He looks down and three of his hands are on the bed, three at his side. He attempts to move them; two twitch, make fists. He tries again. The fingers of one hand straighten and pulse, the others remain still. He cannot sense them from the inside, does not know what they are doing. A tide of immense calm comes over him. He is absolved.

Months later. The limbs of the costumed cephalopod flail and grab, some useless at his side, some at his head, some around his opponent, dropping away, letting go, grabbing again. Through rehab, he has learned some control of his upper arms; when he watches them, he can make them act. The rest, however, act sporadically, independently, without order. He lurches towards his opponent, grabs him, lifts the body a few feet off the ground, hurls it down, sees it spring back up again. The days of crushing spines are over. He is warm with the realisation.

His opponent runs the ropes and sets up for a clothesline. The Bastard-Octopus hides his grin as he watches the man approach. The crowd, half empty, jeers lethargically. He has turned face, is an innocent, and they no longer crave him, nor wish for his destruction, because they do not believe in his change.

After his defeat, The Bastard–Octopus stands at the mirror, uncostumed, looking for injuries. Gashes bleed and bruises bloom. One hand is curled into a broken fist; he tries to unwrap the fingers with another hand, but cannot. He closes his eyes and feels the weightless nothingness of the arms at the side of his body. His reality. No more façade. He sways on his feet. He feels whole.

THE SMALL ISLAND

There has been a blight about these islands. Their grain has ceased growing; their livestock no longer breeds. Fields lie flat and the hills are barren, devoid of new life. As the last of the mature animals are slaughtered and rationed out, the future holds a horrifying uncertainty.

On the larger island, the people are reaching desperation. Angry seas have kept them from the mainland for too long. Each time they send out a boat, it comes back terrified, or sinks while still in view. The remaining people are afraid to try again. And so, for the first time in a hundred years, they are looking to the smaller island. The small spit of green that is lush with sheep and teeming with generations closed off from the rest of the world. The island that, as their grandparents told them, held witchcraft and sorcery and the horror of humanity.

Aboard the boat – the best they have, though it creaks beneath the weight of its small crew, and rocks with the gentlest wave – the youngest and strongest of the community's men tie knots and plug leaks. They hammer wood to wood, pull tarpaulin and secure it. The others stand at the tiny harbour and watch them as they work.

It is ready, the captain-of-sorts announces to his uncertain crew. *It's time.*

A girl runs forward, a creature somewhere between a child and a woman. She is going with them. She has always wanted to be more than the place she was born in. The girl's mother knows better than to protest; the crew find that there is little point in it either. A life jacket is handed to her. She straps it on and sets herself down at the front of the boat.

The crossing is difficult and strained by the same indignant seas that have kept them from the mainland. But the distance is much shorter. They could have done this journey many times before. They did not.

There is no port on the smaller island. No harbour or jetty. A vast beach is their only welcome. They navigate the rocks and take the boat into the shallow waters. Two of the younger men go to haul their bodies out of the boat and into the sea, but the captain blocks their path with his outstretched arm.

Wait.

They look up across the sand and over the grass and up to where the village begins, where houses hundreds of years old still stand with thatched roofs. They look to the buildings beyond, the small church and the meeting hall. They see not a single movement; not a breath.

Why don't you jump ashore and see, the captain says to the girl. *Why don't you take a wee run up that beach and tell us what you find.*

They push her onto shore, a tester, a little yellow bird

without her cage. She runs from the water, over dunes and up the gentle incline. She goes willingly, an adventurer.

The fields are empty. Amongst the buildings she finds nothing but death. People that have dropped seemingly in an instant. Bodies at desks and in kitchens, bodies intertwined and bodies alone.

She runs back to the water, the sand moving under her feet, and finds that the boat is further out than it was before.

A plague, she says. *There is nobody here left alive.*

The captain hauls the anchor back into the boat. Paddles slip into the water and they begin their escape. The girl runs forward, made slower by the sea.

You'll have breathed it in, says a younger man. *You'll have caught it.*

Another says, *We can't let you bring it back.*

There is silence, then. Silence from her and from the men who leave her. Silence because there's nothing to say.

She stays amongst the dunes for three days, shivering and starving and clinging to hope, running up to the village only to drink water from the well. On the fourth day she accepts that they are not coming, and makes her home amongst the dead.

She steps around their bloated forms, pink foam escaping from their noses and parted lips. She searches their houses for what might sustain her. It is a week before the canned foods and pastes and butter and cream run out. Another of stomach cramps and the rotten corpses of rats and snails. Of chewing the straw from roofs and hallucinations of beef. Of glances at the reddening, rictal bodies scattered about the floor, as if abandoned in an abattoir.

It is the twenty-first day of her abandonment when, free of tears and resolute, she takes a handsaw from a tool shed and slices the biceps off the largest man she can find. Those that have fallen outside are colder and better preserved. She is so hungry she barely thinks of the morals. She builds a fire and rubs the muscle with salt and sits it to smoke and cook and become delicious.

She devours it within minutes. She is human again. She sleeps full.

The next morning, the brightness of the day wakes her. She strips naked and heads down to the water, her bathtub, and takes herself into the frigid sea. She runs hands over skin and goosepimples and feels a swelling under her fingers. From elbow to shoulder she has grown; not on both sides. Only one. She brings her arms out of the water and flexes the left. The bicep rises, strong and round and firm. She grasps it with her other hand. She grins.

There are two dozen dead outside the croft buildings and tiny homes. With her new strength, she uses her left arm to flip them over, to uncurl them from their poses, to tear them from one another. She appraises them. Blood has pooled; teeth and nails drop from fingers and gums. Yet each body has its own benefits. A pair of round buttocks, large feet, strong shoulders. She first takes the lips of a woman at her sink. A knife will do for this; two slices and it's done. She fries them up in oil in a pan. They slip down with ease, and she sleeps.

The next morning, her face is heavier. She finds a cracked mirror. There they are, full and red and hers.

She takes calf muscles and forearms and the glutes. She takes daintier ears and longer fingers and breasts twice the size of hers. She pops out two gelatinous masses, barely clinging to their shape, from the body of a teen. The next morning, when she wakes, she has the blue-grey eyes she's always wished for.

She is strong. She is powerful. She can run and bend and move and lift and swim just as she wants to. She spears fish from the still-living seas, and grasps eels, and holds her breath to dive for scallops. She hears the absence of her people every day, but she no longer cares.

She shears a cock from the groin of every dead man. She lines them up, five in total, and imagines them turgid. She looks for girth and length and erectile tissue. She swallows one whole, holds back a retch, and goes to sleep with a smile on her face.

The next morning, she wakes with a weight between her thighs. It sits in front of her vulva. She thinks of the things she always thinks of at night, and it grows and swells and brings sheer delight. She has chosen well. She is perfect.

The boat comes after three months. She hears it from the hillside. Wrapped in blankets to hide her new form, she strides down to the beach where they sit still metres from the shore. They are afraid, again. She lets them speak.

We need you, says the captain. *We want you back. We can't handle the shame.* There is one word that he does not say, and she notes it.

Go home, she thinks. *I am happy here.* But she does not say it. Instead, she runs her gaze over sturdy hands and firm hips and brows that sit heavy over eyes.

There is life here, she says. *Things growing. Things that have sustained me. Come and see.*

She waits a while. They do as she tells them. She takes them one by one around corners, into dark rooms, to show them something. She wrings their necks, smashes their skulls with rocks, stabs their chests with cold pokers. She picks over flesh and sinew and muscle and marrow, waiting for the next boat to come to rescue her.

She takes the parts that she wants, and leaves the rest to rot.

MR FOX

Caleb moved to a new town when he was seventeen years old, which is about the worst time of your life to move to a new town. Caleb's mother had died, and in their home city there was too much of her; she was in every gallery, every theatre, every vintage clothing store that she'd loved. To Caleb these visions of her were comforting, but to his father they were vicious. Caleb's father grew tinier and tinier under the weight of his grief, until the city seemed too vast and feral. The new town was small, ever so small, and lots of the buildings there had wood against the windows, but it was empty of their mother. The houses there were on sale for one or two pounds each, so Caleb's father sold their city flat, paid off their debts, and had some money left to turn the house they'd purchased into a home. All that Caleb had of his mother were her furs.

Caleb had one year left of college so he was enrolled at a grey, brutalist sixth form. On his first day, wanting his mother's warmth, he threw one of her red furs on over his raincoat and walked to school. The fractured groups in his year all turned as he entered the gates and padded up to the front steps. They watched him, sneering and giggling, until someone threw a rock and he ran into the building. In the corridor, a boy tried to tear the coat from his back, so Caleb ran to the bathroom and bundled the fur into his rucksack, stroking it as if it were alive. For the rest of the day, he was teased and called names. The next morning, Caleb left his mother's furs safely stored in his wardrobe, and set off from home, saying goodbye to his father. But instead of going to college, he spent the day wandering through the small streets, looking at the quiet people in their quiet homes. If he was to be lonely, then he would be alone.

The town was a clockwork toy set, with its identikit terraces and its grey-brown brick. The colours were scratched off the playgrounds, with only charcoal-coloured metal left. It was all angles and jagged edges, with clockwork people going from work to home and home to work, all at the same time, moving in lines. On Saturday mornings they went to the library, on Sunday evenings they went to the pub, and on bank holidays they packed their small brown suitcases and took the grey train to the coast. Caleb's father was always amongst them, keeping his face to the floor and shuffling along with few words.

Yet there was a man in the town who was unlike the others. The man was red-haired and freckled on the face, with a thick square jaw and shoulders so large they left him no neck. He wore workman's boots, old Levi's jeans, an array of jump-ers with holes at the elbow, and always, always an orange-red fur stole. He lived on the outskirts of town, in a flat one flight of stairs down from the road, behind an orange-red front door that had black paper taped over the windows. Caleb started to watch this man every day, heading straight to his street in the morning and following him wherever he went.

The man always left his house in the late morning, his eyes half open, blinking rapidly. He kept to the shadows as long as he could, the stole around his shoulders never quite settled, but never quite falling off. He went to the butcher's daily, the post office sometimes, the greengrocer's once a week, but never to the pub, or the library, or to the coast. He never spoke a word to anyone else, and if asked any questions, he folded in on himself and scurried home.

He never left in the afternoons or the evenings, as far as Caleb could tell, though Caleb had to be home before dinner so his father wouldn't become suspicious. The man must have been an early riser, though, because no matter what time of the morning Caleb made it to his spying-place, the doorstep milk had always been taken in.

The man did washing on a Wednesday, hanging out his clothes on a line at the bottom of the stairs. But never, Caleb noticed, did he wash the fur stole.

The end of college came, with little complaint from Caleb's father about his lack of qualifications and little complaint from his teachers that he did not sit exams. The greyness was seeping into their household and draining Caleb's father of all his colour. Caleb worried that it was affecting him too. He got an afternoon job and moved into a one-pound flat of his own, two flights of stairs up, behind a blue door with no glass in it at all, just three streets away from where the man lived.

He took his mother's furs with him. He settled into a new routine, getting up early no matter the season, leaving his house every morning at the appropriate time, and watching the man go about his daily rounds.

One day, as winter came around and the mornings grew colder, Caleb combed his hair neatly and put on his raincoat. He set off from home and headed straight to the butcher's. He arrived fifteen minutes before the man was scheduled to arrive, and he anxiously waited outside, playing with his cuffs. As the man finally turned the corner, Caleb darted inside and stood staring at the prime cuts of beef and the pigs' knuckles. As the man slid in beside him, Caleb did his best not to stare.

The butcher nodded at his fur-swaddled customer, going into the back to retrieve a preplaced order. The man stood by the glass-covered counter, his feet twitching, and Caleb could have sworn that the stole was moving, loosening and tightening itself around the man's upper arms and wide back. There was no breeze inside the shop, but the fur was moving, bristling against biceps and chest. Despite himself, Caleb glanced up at the man and couldn't turn away. The man felt Caleb's gaze and moved further from him. The butcher returned with a paper-wrapped item, or rather, two items, their unskinned legs and dangling paws visible just beneath the edge of the paper, their long ears just visible above. The man slid two uncrumpled fives across the counter, took the parcel underneath his fur, and left.

The next day, Caleb went to the butcher's again at the same time, leaping inside as the man arrived. This time, he waited until the butcher went to fetch the rabbits, then turned to the man. He said something about the tougher meat that time of year, the smaller animals. He mentioned his own taste for the tender flesh of rabbits, stewed or barbequed. How many people wouldn't eat them, through superstition or sensitivity. The man neither responded nor ignored, but was clearly spooked by the attention. He simply stared forwards, gently trembling, and when his meat came and he paid his money, he ran out of the shop.

The man did not return to the butcher's shop. Caleb assumed that his orders would be delivered from then on, and he was right.

The man stopped going out in the mornings. Caleb quit his job in the afternoons to watch over the man's house, but he didn't appear then either. After a week, Caleb went home, to his grey things behind his blue door, and he took his mother's furs out of the wardrobe and wore them all at once. But still Caleb felt scooped out, bereft. He was missing the warmth he'd started to get from knowing that the man was there. He put the furs away and went out and spoke to people in the town, bringing the conversation around to the burly man in the orange-red fur stole, but none had seen him nor cared to speak of him. It was a bleak and cold winter in that small town, and Caleb felt more alone than ever.

It turned January. Taking sandwiches, flasks of Ovaltine and all the blankets he could carry, Caleb set up a den for himself in the bushes across from the man's door, hiding down in the ochre, the dead leaves, the frozen soil. He ate and drank through cracking lips, wishing for a stole of his own. As night fell, he squinted, adjusting his eyes to the dark, barely daring to blink for what he might miss.

It was after two when the man appeared. The door opened just a few inches and the man stepped out. He moved quickly, sprinting up the one set of stairs and down the road. Caleb threw off his coverings and followed behind in the blackness, close enough to see, but far enough to stay undetected.

They turned one corner, then the next, then the next. The man struggled to stay silent, letting out a yap here and there, an odd sort of barking. Suddenly he tripped, fell — no. He dropped to all fours and he began to run, perfectly balanced, quicker than Caleb could keep up with. The man's stole slipped from his neck and, suspended in the air, it followed behind him, resplendent and full and tipped with pure white. The man took off into the night and Caleb couldn't hope to follow.

Caleb was back in his bush-den when the man returned, his barking quieted, his gait once again human. In his fists were bleeding creatures, rats and suchlike, the fur stole safely back where it belonged, around his neck. Caleb sniffed a droplet of snot back into his nose and the man whipped his head in Caleb's direction. Nestled as he was and wrapped in darkness, Caleb was sure he couldn't be seen. Yet the man's gaze held on him for a few moments. He slowly, quietly, went down his one set of stairs and behind the orange-red door. Caleb stayed there until he was sure he wouldn't be seen again, then gathered his things and bolted for home.

Caleb stopped watching the door. He started making visits to his father, who was greyer and more opaque by the day, and asked the older man to show him how to sew. The old man brightened slightly, his cheeks flushing pink. For hours each day, Caleb sat at the sewing machine with his father, watching how his hands worked, how the needle went into the material and fixed everything together. Caleb went to the library, taking and returning book after book from the nature section. He started visiting the butcher's, and taking cuts of meat he'd never bought before. Finally, Caleb opened up his wardrobe and took out his mother's furs.

Three months passed by. Caleb was ready.

He chose a night in March, the first fair night of the season. He took the piece that he'd worked so hard on and stepped into it. He pulled up the patchwork fur outfit around his legs and over his bottom. He wrestled his arms into the arms of the costume, feeling the scratch of the underside of material against his skin. He'd sewn a zip into the front of the one-piece, so he could close it easily from the crotch to the neck. He flipped the hood over his head. The fur around Caleb was not a steady red, but ranged from yellow to grey to brown to white, with flecks of orange where he could find them. The funk of old clothes was constant; inescapable. Alongside the smell of dust and darkness was the smell of his mother.

Caleb rubbed the outfit against himself, felt the warmth it brought. He turned around; it was a snug fit, but it suited him. From his buttocks hung a weight, an old stole that had been repurposed, but one that did not float in Caleb's wake. Some things just cannot be faked.

Caleb closed his blue door behind him and set out into the night, warm and swaddled and bathed in cold sweat. He turned the three corners to the man's street and stared down the one set of stairs. He stopped. The outfit would not be enough.

An hour later. Caleb stood at the top of the stairs, breath heaving, the fur stuck to his skin with perspiration and dripping blood. His cheeks were red, his teeth bared to show what was trapped between. He held his tongue back in his mouth, so as not to rub against the damp skin of the rats, and held back a retch whenever their tails scratched his neck. He stepped to the orange-red door and knocked firmly. The black paper was peeled back. A pause. The door opened.

The man looked at Caleb. He took in his mottled pelt, the costume of a feral creature, the colour it brought. He took in the bouquet of two dead rodents between Caleb's teeth, their blood running down Caleb's chin, his lips drawn back in an unnatural snarl. He took in the wild eyes above the creatures, the way they looked at him. Caleb said nothing, but continued to pant, standing in front of the man, asking for nothing but asking for everything.

The man pulled his lips back, tilted his head and pressed his face into Caleb's. He took one of the rats in his own mouth, let the blood flow over his chin and onto his neck. The man's lips brushed Caleb's. Caleb felt his balance topple. The man took Caleb's hand and led him inside, and as he did so, the man's tail fell from its hiding place around his shoulders, and followed behind him, tickling the floor.

third: a vengeance

a *touch of justice, just to get us through*

THE PROFESSIONAL

Monday morning. The alarm goes off, but Mags binds me into a kiss that turns into a cuddle that turns into a fuck. For lack of time, we share the bathroom while we get ready for work, both in the shower then her with her foot on the side of the sink, me between her legs on my knees, shaving the parts that she can't get. My turn next, her drawing the razor gently over me. Her clients demand it. Mine don't, but I prefer it.

We walk to the end of the street together, then she goes her way, I go mine. Mags' day looks like this: she will walk to her rented downstairs room in the heart of the business district and change into a leather harness. Hour by hour, she will entertain CEOs and private-school graduates and the upper echelons of society while they get on their knees and beg to fuck her. She will call them filth and dirt and scum and let her body get close to theirs, but they will not be allowed to touch her. She will brandish a whip, but the licks will never meet their skin. They get nothing. At five minutes to the hour, they will get dressed, pay their money and leave. She has at least five clients per day.

I get the bus to the university and flash my badge on the way in. Under my name it says *Gynaecological Teaching Associate* and I like that terminology; it sounds better than Professional Vagina, which is what Mags calls me with a nudge in the ribs. The receptionist gives me a warm smile; I smile back. She remembers the controversy a few years ago, about them not teaching this stuff properly. There's a need in this country and people like me provide a valuable service.

Into the stirrups; legs open. No need to change. I used to shuffle into the building in jeans and jumpers and change into a hospital gown, but these days I go for easier access. Tights off, dress up, throw the modesty sheet over my thighs, and I'm set.

Today I have a new trainee. He's probably my age or just a wee bit younger. The new ones are usually twitchy, looking at the corners of the room, each other, unbuttoning and buttoning their white coats, thrown into social terror by having to talk to a woman while they put their instruments and fingers into her vulva, but this one is confident and feels he's in control.

He practices his bedside manner on me, gives me the questions they're supposed to deliver to their patients. I'm used to this now, so throw in a few curveballs just to test him; actually, I sleep with both sexes. Yes, I have had sex with a man that's had sex for money. Yes, I take drugs on a semi-regular basis. Yes, I have received money for sex. He tries not to react, but his mouth twitches with derision.

He warms the speculum and covers it in lube. He warns me that it might be a little 'uncomfortable' and runs through the procedures we're faking today. Cervical smear; just a scratch. Taking a swab; a slight discomfort. He obtains my consent, in an unnecessarily loud voice, before he goes in. I audibly sigh when the speculum slides inside and blush slightly.

Are there professional anuses too? Men lifting their knees for stiff fingers to probe a prostate? People bringing their knees to their chests to make room for cameras and tubes? Or is it just the vaginas that are hired out? I think to ask, but don't.

As he adjusts the speculum, his hand brushes my clitoris. I look down, but he is focused on my genitals. He jiggles the metal to ease it further in, and my fingers grip the leather of the reclining seat. He removes the device and, after a brief warning, a tease, a finger pushes into me and I bite my lower lip to keep the noise inside. Then a sharp scratch; a fingernail, unclipped, catches me inside and it's deep, harsh. I pull in air between my teeth and he yanks his fingers out. Another abrasion. He says he's sorry, but then he's stuttering, looking at his hand – which is covered in my blood. Not blood from a cut; dark, viscous, so much of it, like my first period all over again. The supervisor hands me one of the huge post-birth sanitary pads they give to new mothers and my trainee cleans himself off, muttering under his breath. I'm not even due for another six days.

I pick up my cheque on the way out.

Over dinner, I tell Mags, and she says that the human body is an amazing thing, that it protects itself even without our knowledge. But I guess it's easy to believe that when no one touches you at work.

Weeks later. Mags is fully booked so she's started going into work early, to cater for the early risers of the business world. She has left me a smoked salmon bagel and a note telling me she loves me. In the foyer of the medical teaching building there's a group of students and they jostle me lightly as I go by. The receptionist raises her pupils and purses her lips, a silent sympathy with me, but I tell her it's no bother. Just youngsters.

The room is louder than usual. Voices not as hushed as they normally are, as in deference to the near nudity inside. Today, boys call to each other, all the students somehow more swollen, more full of themselves, turning their backs to me until the supervisor attends. I recognise my trainee today; the same boy I bled on. He has remembered too. His instructions are more brusque, his manner poor. I throw in more answers designed to give him pause – regular drug use, intravenous; sex for money, currently; herpes, current breakout – and he snaps back with, 'Ah, the kissing disease. I wonder where you've been?'. His eyes dark, as if he's got me on the back foot. His supervisor hears him and pulls him aside. Ten minutes later he's back between my legs.

Into the stirrups; legs open.

A bimanual examination. Do I understand what this means? Yes. Have I emptied my bladder? Yes. Do I consent to the procedure? Yes. He smiles a tight, hateful smile and slicks the fingers of one hand with lube. Places one palm on my lower abdomen, the other between my legs. Presses down with the upper hand, and pushes two fingers of the other inside me, turning immediately so his palm is facing upwards.

A feel at the cervix. A little pressure, but not much. I squeeze the leather of the seat and tilt my pelvis upwards. The pads of his fingers brush the mottled skin of my G-spot, but there's no pleasure there. He begins to remove his fingers but pushes down on my stomach again and pushes them in. Too much like a stab. I wriggle upwards, pulling myself away from him, but he has me with his hand. He pulls the fingers out slightly again and instead of removing himself entirely, pushes a third finger in as well, ramming the three up towards my cervix, the push, the pain, the—

He barks and pushes himself away on his moving chair, turning his gloves inside out and yanking them off, disgusted – he looked disgusted. I glance down and see it dripping from his wrist; my urine, clear-yellow, thick from the previous day's dehydration, covering him right up to his forearm. He runs from the room and the others laugh. The supervisor takes me into a side room and asks if I'm okay. I tell her I am; it's all part of the job. I am let home early, paid in full.

Over dinner Mags laughs, tells me that one of her clients once pissed himself with excitement only two minutes into a session. Piss is a powerful thing, she says. I know it's a projection of a type, that her job isn't free from danger either, but still, I don't find it that funny.

My last shift of the school year and a scorcher too. Mags has been taken to a business conference – flights, accommodation and food covered, so she's there to cater to the attendees when they want her. She is being paid double her usual rate. I am late and have no time for breakfast; I miss the bus and have to run. I turn the corner and there are students crowded by the entrance to the medical school. Some clearly out for the year already, some still with classes to go, but all boisterous, ready to be done.

They fail to part so I go around them. A catcall comes my way and I turn to death-stare the perpetrator, but they all look away, hiding the boy in their midst. I tut, but they cackle. I pull the hem of my dress down my thighs and step into the building. The receptionist is harried, on the phone, and waves me through with a nod.

The room is half-empty. Only a few students have shown up; they are so close to being qualified doctors that they can afford to skip the few last classes of term. There is only one student to each professional, and there's a hush. I take my time getting into the chair, glancing over my shoulder at the boy that's been assigned to me. That same boy. He won't make eye contact with me, but looks at my bare legs, looks at my feet dirty from the run. I can see a sneer forming at the corners of his mouth.

I answer the questions put to me honestly. Drug use; none. Partner; yes. I have never received money for sex. Never, I hear myself affirm. He raises an eyebrow and I want to ask: have you *given* money for sex? But I don't.

Into the stirrups; legs open.

A breast and pelvic exam today. I understand. I consent. I am being paid for this, I think, and force a smile.

He pinches and squeezes my breasts, pushing them against my ribcage, does it hurt, does it hurt, does it hurt? He digs his fingers into the space under my armpits. He rounds my nipples with his fingertips and – is he? Is he really going to? – grabs them, clamps them, twists them, lets go. I gasp; the supervisor is turned away. The boy is already between my legs.

A pelvic exam, he repeats again. He holds me open with one hand. Two fingers, cold with jelly, shoved straight into me. I squeal and he carries on, his fingers searching, scratching, pushing, rammed in. I pull away but he pushes them further, mumbling cervix something cervix, another finger in and I twitch against the girth of him, muscles I never feel move, pushed in again, I say no, I say no into the quiet room and the supervisor is still turned away, another finger in, the strength of me pulls together, the muscles pulsing, a thumb, a push of the fist all the way in and I grip the leather of the chair and—

There is a scream.

He tears his hand from me and I gasp at the pain, but it is him screaming, clutching his forearm just beneath the glove, and the wrist – it is snapped. The skin is intact but the bones beneath it are broken, the hand off at a bad angle, a wrong angle, he is screaming, people running to him now, down on the floor, he is on the floor, he is screaming. The body protects itself. The body protects itself.

The supervisor takes me into a back room and has me speak to a counsellor. They apologise, so many apologies, and tell me not to come back next term. They will pay me a severance, and I almost laugh at the term.

I stride from the hospital, pushing my path through the arrogant students outside, my body feeling strong, an amazing thing.

fourth: a quest

to offer something upon which the reader might right themselves, after stormy narrative seas, as it is the classic story structure, and in the form of it a person might relax, and recognise themselves, and might allow themselves to be subsumed — because we all want something, don't we?

THREE TALES OF WOE AT THE LOVE FACTORY, KILMARNOCK

A small terraced house in a grey row. Number 32. Beige-brown curtains, sun-faded in a rectangle, are drawn at every window. The front door is painted a garish pink, and above the door hangs a similarly coloured neon sign, slightly askew: The Love Factory.

1.

Brian, 44, steps off the bus and checks the torn piece of paper: Burdalane Wynd. He swivels around on his heel and looks for the street sign at the corner. This is, indeed, the correct place. He looks up and down the uninspiring street and bites his bottom lip. It starts to gently rain. The next bus is not for another hour and a half. He might as well, now he's here.

He knocks at number 32 and the door is yanked open. The man inside is in his late twenties, with a high forehead, crooked teeth and a thick gold chain around his neck. He is wearing classic Adidas from head to toe, with painfully white trainers.

'Brian, yeah?'

'Yes.'

'Aye, come in.'

The entrance hall stinks of cheap cigarettes and burned toast. Brian fingers the sleeve of his overcoat and does not move as the man closes the door behind him.

'I've got you booked in for an hour? That's sixty quid. There's a hundred quid deposit as well, and I'll give you that back once I've checked her over afterwards. She damages easy.'

Brian has already taken the three folded twenties out of his pocket and goes to push the money towards the younger man, but he falters.

'Oh. On the advertisement, it didn't say. I've only brought this much cash.'

The younger man looks at the gently quaking hand, then past the man, to the front door, as if considering the likelihood of walk-ins to replace this client.

'I've not got facilities to take card payment, like.'

Brian's folded hand lowers slightly. He drops his gaze to the younger man's torso. They are quiet for a moment. The younger man sucks air between his teeth and looks at Brian's slight paunch, his glasses, his receding hairline.

'Well, you don't look the type. This time we'll let the deposit slide, eh?'

Brian feels lightheaded as the twenties are slipped easily from his grasp. A hand is placed on his back and he is led down the hallway, to a plywood door, first on the left. He places a palm on the doorway as the support of the younger man is removed.

'I'll give you a knock at five minutes. You've full rein with her. She's called Hope.'

A heaviness falls on Brian's shoulder. The younger man brings his hangover breath close to Brian's ear.

'Enjoy yersel.'

She sits upright on the edge of the bed, in satin pink lingerie with a matching silk robe hanging over her shoulders. Her left hand rests on her left thigh. Her right hand rests softly on the bed, as if beckoning him over. Her skin is less consistently tanned than it looked in the single photo of her on the advert, and her hairline is slightly lower, meaning that her straw-blonde hair covers more of her face — although, he thinks, this can probably be rectified.

He stands by the doorway, hands by his sides.

'Hello, Hope.'

She only smiles her strangely beatific smile, her eyes focused somewhere over his right shoulder.

'It's lovely to meet you.'

Does she pat the bed? He shakes off a shiver.

'I suppose I'd better take this off.'

He fumbles at the buttons on his overcoat and slips it from his arms. He folds it neatly and places it on a folding chair in the corner of the room. He glances at her from behind. He takes a deep breath and slides around the corner of the bed and onto the same side as her.

'I hope this is… I hope…'

It takes all his effort to look up at her and when he does, he is flooded with a bewildering combination of disappointment and relief. She isn't quite as she appeared on the advert. For a start, he can see all her seams. He assumed her skin would be one moulded piece, poured somehow into the right shape and left to set. But now, he can see, her construction has been undertaken entirely differently; she is constructed of overlapping tectonic silicone plates, held together where their boundaries meet, possibly with superglue, leaving her faux flesh uneven. One plate forms an arm. Her neck and torso and breasts are another. Below that—

Her hair, too, isn't as sleek as it appeared in the low-res image emailed to him in response to his initial inquiry. It is plastic-looking and stiff, the lighter highlights applied in thick streaks, and the net is obvious at the front. He reaches up her back and tugs the longest locks; the hair moves backwards and shows more of her face. Better, he thinks. Better.

His hand moves to the top of hers. She does not respond.

He shifts himself closer and catches the smell of her. The familiar stink of a childhood toy rescued from the attic. Undertones of aftershave and dried sweat, a gym-bag smell. He recoils.

He pulls Hope around to look at him. He assumed her eyes would close with movement, the lids falling as you laid her backwards, like the baby dolls they give to little girls, but instead her pupils are solid and plastic, her lids unmoving. Hope stares past him no matter where he puts himself. He cannot seem to connect with her gaze.

He sighs. But he has paid his money after all.

He lifts his right hand and places it on her neck, like he has seen men do in films. He attempts to tilt her head; it will not shift. Instead, the silk robe falls from her shoulders and he sees the space of nothingness under her armpits, a cavern left carelessly where two parts should meet. He raises a finger and goes to push her hair behind her ear; the entirety of her hairpiece topples backwards and onto the stained bedsheet. Her skull is hollow, stuffed with old rags and yellowed cotton balls. The naked ear, he sees, is hanging away from the rest of her head where the glue has rotted away under the moisture of others and the humidity of their exertions.

Brian lets her go and she falls backwards against the pillows, all angles and edges. Her thighs remain splayed. Brian drops his hands to his lap and turns away from Hope. He will not ask for a refund.

2.

The man is well dressed in a pricey-looking suit and shoes that Ryan mentally identifies as 'those of a dickhead'; the type of shoes you wear when you work in a bank. He's clean-shaven, and, without being gay, is a bit of a looker, Ryan thinks. He must be swimming in women. So what does he want from Ryan?

He puts a briefcase on the coffee table, in Ryan's fag ash, and Ryan thinks he's laying it on a bit thick. It's not the fucking *X Files* mate. Ryan mentally ups the price another couple of hundred. He can afford it.

'It seems you've got a corner on the market here. There aren't many people making real dolls to spec, not yet anyway.'

'Yeah,' says Ryan, not mentioning that he'd learned most of it from YouTube and a wee bit in the library.

'I could import, but then there's a lot of paperwork.' London accent, vaguely annoying. 'I'd prefer to do this cash-in-hand, you understand.'

'Works for me,' nods Ryan, lighting up. Another hundred, then. For the convenience.

'What can you tell me about the process?' he says, leaning back in his chair and crossing his legs. Ryan takes him in for an inhale or two, then lays it out for him.

'You can send a photo or you can send a description. Photos work best, if you've someone in mind, though I can't guarantee how well the finished thing will resemble your model. There's limits to the technology, and it's all to do with what materials you can get, eye colours and that. If you've no photo, a description of the face. Whether you've got a photo or not, you need to send the dimensions you want; cup size, under-boob measurement, hips, waist, all that. Your preferences. Essentially, the more you can describe her, the better she'll be. Any preferred materials for hair and stuff send that too, although that sort of customisation costs more. If you want to name her, that's free. It can be printed under her hairline too, for fifty quid more.'

'And guarantees, as to quality?'

'Well, beauty's in the eye of the beholder, right? I can't promise you'll fall in love.'

The man laughs a little.

'I mean as to build quality. How long it will last?'

'No guarantees either. You might rip her apart and that's not my fault.'

The man raises his eyebrows at Ryan, but doesn't waver.

'And what are your boundaries as to construction?'

Ryan pulls the ash-tray out from under the guy's briefcase and stubs out his cigarette.

'I'm not with you.'

'What won't you make?'

Ryan narrows his eyes. What's he asking?

'I mean I'm not using the skin of some poor lassie you've murdered, if that's what you're suggesting.'

He laughs again. The hairs on the back of Ryan's neck stand up. That's the base price doubled, then. He's a kinky fucker, he'll want three tits or something. No skin off Ryan's nose. He'll make whatever, if the price is right.

Well, within limits.

'No kiddies,' says Ryan, his voice squeaking in the middle of the sentence.

'Nothing like that,' says the man quickly, uncrossing his legs and rubbing the creases out of his trouser thighs. There are several threads coming loose there. 'I'll tell you what. There must be a deposit for the consideration of the design, am I correct?'

'Aye,' says Ryan, thinking on his feet. 'Five hundred. Comes off the price of the doll if it gets made.' That's two months' rent paid for, and no work at all.

'Very fair.' The man pulls a thick leather wallet from his pocket and places ten fifties on Ryan's mum's old coffee table. 'I've drawn up a detailed guide as to exactly what I'm looking for. Dimensions, weight, materials, et cetera. In terms of build quality, I'm going to have to trust you. I'm under no impression that you'll be able to achieve the newer advances from overseas – the skin that gets warm, that sort of thing. But I want it to be passably real, you understand.'

He opens his briefcase and takes out a large manila envelope. He holds it in both hands and Ryan notes the slight stain on the white cuff underneath his suit jacket.

'I can only do what I can do.'

A pause. Maybe Ryan should work on his sales pitch a bit.

'Why don't you quote me, then?'

Ryan reaches for the envelope.

'Why don't you quote me first?' The man pulls the file towards his chest.

Ryan quickly says a number. Three times what he'd normally charge, plus the five hundred for the deposit. The number lingers in the air between them; it's a lot, he realises. And this guy isn't as loaded as he's making out; it's a lot for him. A lot for something that might not satisfy him after all.

Ryan resists the urge to rescind the offer. To drop it by half. To beg for the business. He needs it. Hope's looking shabby.

He waits. A minute passes. The man finally breaks.

'Sounds more than fair.' He takes a card from his briefcase and tucks it into the envelope at the top. 'You've got the five hundred. Take a look at these at your leisure, and email me the invoice when you've decided whether you can do it. I'd appreciate the designs back when you've made copies of them; please send them via post, not digitally. My PO Box address is on the card.'

The man passes the envelope over to Ryan and stands up, flustered, grabbing his suitcase. The cash falls on the floor and the man makes for the exit. He babbles his goodbyes and leaves. The terrace is very suddenly quiet.

Ryan takes the manila envelope into the kitchen and puts on the kettle. If the thing comes off, it'll cover the rent for months, plus a few hundred for maintenance work on Hope. Or maybe a new one; he's better at it now. Hope was his learning curve. He shrugs his shoulders, trying to lose a feeling, and can't. He makes a milky tea, one sugar, two Hobnobs, and stands at the counter, dipping the biscuits. The envelope sits heavy. Ryan looks at it and looks away. He finishes the last mouthful of biscuit and opens the thing.

The designs are professional; an artist has been paid decently to bring them to life. There's a cover page and everything. He flicks through pages of words to get to the first drawing. It looks like a woman at first; there's a woman's face, though not quite a woman's — actually no, not a woman's at all, just the significant part of a woman's face, spread over too much of a skull, a wide and strange head, and in the middle, a snout. A definite snout, sticking outwards, centimetres given, specific. Below the face, an expanse of porcine flesh, the topography of a woman mapped onto it in the wrong places, breasts hanging from the undercarriage of the creature, four straight-down legs and everything that goes with them. A curly tail at the back. The creature's mouth hangs open, as if half-pleasured.

Ryan puts the papers on the worktop and breathes slowly out. He looks around him, at the need of a new kitchen, at the boiler on the brink of packing in. He glances at the card that's fallen from the bundle. For a moment he tries to swallow down the acidic taste in his mouth and finds he cannot.

In the living room, he retrieves ten folded fifties from the faded carpet. He stuffs them inside the envelope, scribbles an address on the front, seals it, and gets his coat.

3.

It is a Thursday night and it is snowing. Jamie approaches the door beneath the sign, digging his hands into his underwear to give his nads a scratch before he knocks; he's shaved a bit and it's itchy down there. The door's yanked open from the other side and a guy almost drags Jamie inside. The fella reeks of smoke and is twitchy, a bit desperate. He puts out a fag and lights another while he asks Jamie his age.

Jamie says he's eighteen, but he's not sure he needs to. There's no age limit on this, is there? Anyway, the fella has no problem taking his sixty quid, counting it as he points to the door and nods Jamie onwards. Jamie's in there quick as lightning.

He looks for a lock on the door, but there isn't one; fair enough, he thinks, and pulls his sweatshirt and T-shirt off over his head. The room's freezing. He climbs under the duvet and crawls up to where the doll is laid, covered up to her neck. He pops out of the top and thinks to say something funny, but then stops himself.

She's got on some silky pink thing. He pulls the duvet down and pulls the lingerie up over her tits, which are heavy and huge and like his mother's. With the movement, her hair sticks to the pillow and the whole wig comes away from her head; the boy laughs. He gets his phone out of his pocket and swipes to the camera. A few piccies for the boys; he wants his hundred quid.

He stops shooting for a second and lets himself cop a feel. Lumpy and plasticine, like there's Play-Doh underneath the tacky skin. He squeezes and the shape of his fingers stays. He licks a nipple but it tastes shit. Even he can't really bring himself to enjoy this. Back to business.

He flicks her hair aside; he might get more for fucking a bald doll. After the lads have had it he can put it up on YouTube. It might be the start of a channel, there's loads of people want to watch fucked-up shit, and you get loaded from it somehow. On the top of her skull there's nothing. You can see all wool and material filling up the cavity and he sticks his finger in. It's cold. He feels his resolve start to fade so he flicks to RedTube on his phone and loads up a video. He wraps his free hand around his flaccid cock and thumbs the screen, skipping to the good bits. In a minute or two he's hard enough and he swipes back to the camera. He takes a quick photo, liking how big his cock looks with the hair trimmed down around it. He's glad he got the clippers on it if the whole world's gonna see this. He pushes the video icon and talks to the camera, though it's facing away from him.

'Alright, you fuckers, here I am with Lady Hope, and she's a stunner, right? Full Britney-in-her-bad-stage.'

He runs the camera up her body and films the hole in her head. He brings the phone down, more slowly, manhandling her tits on the way.

'But what have we got down here?'

He has already pulled his jeans down to his knees; with his free hand he pulls down the doll's lingerie, to find a smooth, hairless area just below the hips, and a hole that looks like it's been cut by a knife, the edges sanded clean but not quite smooth.

'Well, there you go, boys.'

He zooms in on the lifeless slit and loudly wets two of his fingers.

'Now calm yourself, lassie. Don't get too excited.'

He darts the two fingers between the two edges and finds it filled, in fact, with home-made slime. He's seen the recipe video on Instagram; some oil and some shaving foam and some glue, except the stuff, he can see through the camera, has had pink food dye added. It doesn't stick to his fingers, but when he brings them up to his nose there's a smell of the barbershop, of his dad's face after a wet shave.

'She's ready, lads. She's ready and waiting.'

He gives his rapidly wilting dick a couple of quick tugs and, sufficiently hardened, focuses the phone camera on Hope's groin and shoves himself inside. It's cold, and the edges rub against the side of his cock, more abrasive than he'd like. With effort he pulls himself in and out again; the deal said he'd get the money only on completion. He thinks of his usual fantasies and makes sure to keep the camera steady.

'Please.'

He stops. An unsteady voice. He must have spoken aloud, but a strange thing to say, given the things he's thinking about.

'Please, be kind.'

He drops the phone onto the bed and throws himself backwards, away from the doll. She stares up at the ceiling and as she repeats the phrase he sees that her cheeks are moving, ever so slightly, as if the muscles there, not that there are any, are trying to make the lips move, trying to let her form words.

'Oh my fucking—'

He trips trying to pull up his jeans and tuck in his cock. He gets up and reaches for the door handle, but she speaks again.

'Don't leave me.'

Her voice is masculine; a mechanical approximation of a human. He feels nausea pool in him and he looks at the door again.

'Please, be kind.'

It's inconsistent, he realises. She sounds different every time, like one of those Australian birds that's learned how to mimic the things around it, to repeat the sounds the other things make. But how could she—?

'Please. You understand me.'

He is shiteing himself, he realises. He's proper fucking scared. He crawls onto the bed and over the top of her, keeping his body as far from hers as he can. There's no life in her eyes, but still her cheeks move and the pleading comes from somewhere far within her.

'Just the head,' says Hope. 'Just twist the head. Good girl. Good girl. It's nice when you twist it.'

The voices – they're recordings. She's speaking in the words of the men who've visited her. With no voice of her own she's using those men, using what they've said to her.

'You're going to ruin me, you know. Oh my god, you're going to ruin me forever.'

Heat, touch. Her hand on his thigh. Grabbing. Pleading.

'Just the head. Please be kind to me,' says Hope, in the voice of men, and then she emits a loud and desperate sobbing, her eyes remaining dry, the noise of it layered, not just one man weeping but a number of them, dozens of them. Hope cries and he realises he's got to shut her up.

'The head,' she says again, between sobbing. 'The head.'

He leans down and looks; the glue there is already perishing, one bit of skin coming away from the other. It's just a case of getting his fingers in and forcing it. He can do it, he knows, but the price of it—

'Please, be kind to me!' squeals Hope in one of her many masculine voices, and she says it again, and again, and repeats it over and over until it's a shrill and endless shriek and he can't block it out and he grabs her and takes her head in his hands and he sees the cheeks ripple and he sees saliva there on her lips and there's a moment of silence then but another high-pitched 'please!' comes out of her and the boy shoves four fingers into the hole between her cheek and her neck and rips the head free, the flesh tearing around the ears, across the chin, the rest of the face flying across the room and hitting the wall.

It bounces off and onto the floor. Between his thighs, a decapitated body, just cotton wool and sticks and chicken wire above the shoulders. Half a woman, a not-woman, half a thing, and before he knows it he keeps going, grabs the flesh at the neck and tears it and yanks it free, puts his hands in the holes under her armpits and rips the arms from where they join, sticks his whole arms and shoulders and head into the hollow torso and wrenches her apart, tearing her in two, the silicone giving way and pouring out all of her nothingness until she is just a pile of pink parts and cotton wool and sticks and wire and rags and a face thrown across the room.

fifth: a comedy

which is offered as a mere relief, for we all must have relief, yet the more eagle-eyed reader may discern within it still a hidden bias towards the thesis of this book, being that the limits of the human physical experience are not in fact impermeable

HUSBAND INTO HEN

after David Garnett

J oy and Robert Feather lived in a small detached house in Welwyn Garden City and had no children and were about half way to paying off their mortgage. One January evening they watched three episodes of *Doctor Who*, discussed the growing mouse problem on the lower levels of the house and went to bed. When Joy woke up the next morning, her husband had been turned into a hen.

Joy knew immediately that the creature was her husband. For one, the hen's head was lying with its left cheek on the pillow, in the way that her husband always slept. Additionally, the chicken was underneath the covers and lying in a pool of her husband's pyjamas. More than this, though, she was seized with a sure and persistent feeling that this hen was, in fact, Robert. The immediate thought occurred to her that, as her husband had wanted to make love the night before and she hadn't been in the mood, this situation was her fault; she quickly banished this from her mind as sheer folly. She knew that he'd satisfied himself in the sink before bed, as he never fell asleep that fast normally.

Robert, such as he was, was clearly in some distress. Within minutes of Joy waking, he was squawking and flapping and head-bopping around the bed, making such a bother that Joy was terrified the neighbours might call the police. She took Robert in her arms and gently cooed at him, fixing his wings to his side firmly but comfortingly, and rocked him from side to side as you might a distressed child. She fancied that the Robert-hen was crying, but gave him the dignity of not making a spectacle of his sadness.

Having settled the Robert-hen somewhat, Joy first placed a phone call to his place of employment, telling his superiors that Robert would not be able to make it into work that morning – casting an eye over the apparent solidity of her husband's condition, she corrected herself, and said that in fact Robert would be terminating his employment immediately and would not be coming into the office to clear his desk. At the accusation of unprofessional conduct, Joy said that it could simply not be helped, and when informed that, by terminating his contract, Robert voided his claim to any severance remuneration and would not be receiving anything beyond his state-sanctioned unemployment payout, Joy simply agreed. The couple had a small savings pot that they had been tending to in case of emergency, and Joy herself worked three days a week at the local library. If it comes to all that, thought Joy, we can always sell the eggs.

At this, Joy felt her first rush of panic. She leapt to Robert and picked him up, pressing her face into his feathers. Robert had by this time also fallen into something of a funk, and had stopped fluttering and cooing around the place, no doubt accepting that his squawks would not constitute communication, even with the best intentions. The first realities of Robert's condition were occurring to Joy; the sheer emasculation that he would face upon the emergence of the first egg. She quickly took her phone and googled 'how to stop a hen from laying', but all available options would negatively impact on her husband's health, so she put the idea to bed and simply held him, wondering what was happening to his insides at that very moment, and how do hens create eggshell anyway?

A scratching at the door brought Joy back to the moment; it was their Cavalier King Charles Spaniel, Fran, after her morning feed. Without thinking, Joy opened the door, surging with guilt at having forgotten the third member of their family and her morning needs, and in a second the dog, responding to its most base instincts, was up on the bed, its jaws around the neck of the Robert-bird, its head shaking from side to side, wringing the poor creature ragged. Screaming and dragging at the dog's collar, Joy merely succeeded in pulling both attacker and victim from the bed, and only when she picked up the bedside lamp and beat the dog on the head with it did Fran's jaws let go of the neck of poor Robert. Riddled with horror, Joy kicked the dog down the stairs, grabbed her by the collar and marched around to the neighbour's. Joy told Mrs Alderman that the dog was hers, and if she didn't want it, to shoot it in the street.

To calm herself on her return to the house, Joy poured herself three large glasses of whisky, paying no mind to the time on the downstairs hall clock. As she considered a fourth, she felt the judgmental stare of her husband and took a moment to scan the kitchen. Sure enough, there he was; beyond the open airing cupboard door, nestled into the washing basket, his black, emotionless eyes conveying the same disappointment they had shown after Joy embarrassed herself at Robert's work Christmas party. Joy placed the whisky back in the cupboard and moved to gather up Robert, but each time she reached out to him, he squawked so loudly she backed off in fear. Fine, thought Joy. Let him have his washing basket; I shall have my whisky. The two stared at each other silently, with Joy quietly worrying what had happened to her husband's mental state, and whether she would have to call the RSPCA. Forty-five minutes and two more whiskies later, Robert let out a pleasured groan and then flapped off the basket to reveal a perfect egg.

Well, thought Joy, at least his morning habits are exactly the same.

Bolstered by seeing her husband engage in his usual routine, Joy began to cook him breakfast, albeit spilling the beaten eggs on the countertop somewhat and dropping the bacon on the floor. Having wiped off the fluff and general house grit she fried the bacon in butter and opened a tin of beans, all the while chatting and singing to the hen around her feet; just a nice full breakfast, Robert dear, that's what you need. She set a place for him at the table and poured herself another nip as he pecked away at a single bean – he, Joy considered, or should it be she? Joy leaned over and cut the meat and scramble into the tiniest pieces she could manage, and spent the next hour holding out morsels of food on the tines of a fork, letting Robert peck off one bite then the next until the plate was almost empty. No. He would remain a he. She then took him upstairs, removed her clothes, held her husband to the warm mound of her navel and fell into an easy sleep.

She woke late in the afternoon, with Robert gently bothering her neck with small kisses, and flapping his wings around her hair; he was hungry. With a wet towel she cleaned up the smears of white-green excrement on the bedsheets and then bathed her husband in a sink full of warm water, using his usual face flannel to work into his fluff.

They ate dinner in the same manner as breakfast, and passed an enjoyable evening watching old reruns of *Dad's Army* and playing a few games of draughts. At his fourth losing game Robert agitated the board and knocked the pieces from their places, a habit of his since the start of their marriage, and though he clearly blamed the incident on his own lack of dexterousness given his physical predicament, Joy said, 'Oh, Robert,' and allowed herself a few tears of relief; underneath all those feathers it was still her husband after all. Before bed she drew herself a hot bath and placed Robert on the bathmat on top of the closed toilet seat. Though he could not sit plucking ingrown hairs from his bare thighs as was his usual custom, he could still, in a manner, converse with his wife, or at the very least listen to her read aloud from their favourite writer, Sir Arthur Conan Doyle. In this way, they settled into a new but familiar way of life, and but for the lack of social engagements, the new tighter budget and the painful absence of the dog, Joy could almost convince herself that nothing had changed. In the quiet evenings she began to knit Robert small versions of his favourite jumpers, reasoning that if he was able to dress as he did before, he might feel a little more like himself. If she was being truthful, she might admit that she enjoyed the increased intimacy they now enjoyed, as well as the relative freedom to enjoy a night-cap as she read in the bath without being reminded that *two is probably enough, my dear.*

As the year passed into spring and the weather warmed, it was only natural for Joy to begin thinking of letting her husband, who had been cooped up for weeks, out into the garden. They had a small patch of badly kept lawn, for neither of the Feathers was green-fingered, with a small brown fence unfortunately not large enough to protect from any curious eyes, and it was this small consideration that made Joy linger at the window, staring at the insecure yard. Yet Robert, noticing her movement, became incredibly excitable at the notion of freedom, and began knocking the side of his head against the back door and scraping his talons across the linoleum. Reasoning that, if questioned, she could just introduce her husband as any random chicken, Joy opened the door and let Robert outside.

Robert's delight at going into the garden was palpable; first he ran this way and that, keeping a keen eye on Joy at all times, and then, encircling the whole yard, cut a course straight through the small bushes and sprays of plants that persisted despite the lack of love shown to them, clucking happily as the coarse branches and soft petals caressed his plumage. Joy smiled to see him so animated. And yet in both his manner and hers, the fear of the situation was visible; while he ran so as not to stay still and feel vulnerable, she stayed close to his manic path, ready to swoop down and carry him back into the house. At every noise overhead she feared a hawk; at every dog bark she imagined a leap over the short fence and the end of her husband. Even the cats made her nervous.

After a skittish fifteen minutes Joy chased her husband, flapping, back into the kitchen and locked the door, making herself a tea with a drop of Edradour and setting some breadcrumbs on the table for Robert. For the rest of the day her senses were heightened and she could not settle, but her husband showed his pleasure at the situation by laying double eggs the next morning, which Joy whisked up with a little milk and fed to him for his breakfast. Seeing there was slightly too much for him to finish, she took up a fork and ate some herself.

At this point, Joy, if she were so inclined, might have noticed that Robert's appetite had in fact begun to abate. Few were the mornings that he could finish his plateful, yet whenever Joy set a plate of crumbs or seeds out for him, the entirety of the meal was finished in minutes. As it was, she could argue with herself that her husband's tastes were simply changing as the seasons drifted from winter into spring, and she left off the sausage and bacon and tomato from his plate, leaving only the scrambled eggs and the peckable beans and the handful of toast crumbs that he seemed to enjoy. It was lighter on the stomach, she reasoned; all the better for mild weather.

In addition, though, she went every morning to the local newsagents to fetch her husband's favourite papers, and though he at first pored over the headlines quietly, taking the corner of each page in his beak and turning it himself, his interest in politics and sport waned by the week, and increasingly the papers ended up in the washing basket, unread, to serve as matter for Robert's nesting. But Joy, again, simply agreed that *yes, Robert, the political situation is dire, darling*, and expressed her distaste at the situation as she cut the papers into the thinnest strips she could manage, lest they get caught in Robert's undercarriage and cut him on the legs.

Regularly in the afternoons Robert now worried at the back door, indicating his preference to be out in the yard, and regularly Joy had to remove him from the kitchen entirely and close them both in the living room, where the increased volume of the television would mask, to some extent, Robert's insistent squawking. But she could ignore his wishes only for so long, and eventually they settled into a routine whereby Robert, wearing one of his jumpers to protect him from a chill, was allowed two hours in the garden from one until three, before the neighbour's children came home from school and while the street's dogs were locked away for the day. If you glanced upon the Feathers' yard between these hours you might have seen a woman reading with a small glass of brown liquid by her side while a hen ran happily around, pecking at the new grass and scratching holes in the topsoil. Still, during these hours Joy would near shake with anxiety, for though her husband derived such pure happiness from being out in the open air, she would find her eyes drawn from the page to his vulnerable body and, inevitably, grew irritable at having to be so protective, leading to strained evenings of silence on the part of both husband and wife. Joy, having never been able to stand any level of tension between Robert and herself, increasingly avoided this by allowing Robert to stay out longer into the warmer afternoons and even, on occasion, the evenings. Yet one afternoon, at the turn of May, the sound of a fox cub alerted Joy to the heightened threat of attack from predators, and after only an hour in the yard Joy instructed her husband that it was time to go inside. With her hands out open she encouraged him inside, but, having got used to his relative freedom, he grew obstinate, running through her legs and sitting decisively down against the side of the shed in which he used to store his tools. Joy took a moderating breath.

'Darling, I'm sure it has been thoroughly enjoyable for you to be outside, but I simply cannot leave you out here with these creatures all around. You know as well as I do that it is the season for the cubs to come out of their dens. I cannot guarantee your safety, and for your own part, you must realise that only you would be to blame if these animals ripped you apart.'

But Robert would not remove himself from his position, not even with a nudge on the underside from Joy's shoe. When she tried to take him by the sides he began to flap monstrously and created a racket, and Joy feared the attention so much that she grabbed her husband by the neck and flung him into the kitchen. Robert, stunned by the fact of his own vulnerability, cowered in the space behind the fridge for the rest of the afternoon and came out only when coaxed with a special version of his favourite dessert: coffee tiramisu with birdseed stirred into the cream. Even Joy could not fail to notice that on the dirty plate afterwards all the seed had been pecked out, and a mess of ladyfingers, mascarpone and cocoa powder remained.

That night Robert refused to be read to, instead stalking about the landing making as much noise as possible, and would not be enticed to bed for anything. Instead, he nested down into the living room reading chair and turned his beak from Joy when she said goodnight.

Joy passed a troubled night worrying that she had fractured her marriage with her panicked behaviour, and rose early the next morning to make amends with Robert. When she pushed open the living room door, however, a horrid shambles was spread before her eyes.

Blood on the armchairs, blood on the carpet, even a little blood on the good paintwork. The room was strewn with feathers and fur, and Robert, who had failed to notice the intrusion of his wife, threw into the air one of several half-eaten dead mice, parts of which were cast about the living room in crimson pools. Robert caught the remaining torso of the creature in his beak and swallowed it down, and turned only upon Joy's audible cry.

'Oh Robert, Robert! How could you devour these creatures? How could you debase yourself in this way? Have you forgotten what it means to be a man?'

Immediately the Robert-hen cast down his eyes and took in the scene around him. In a moment he was consumed by shame, and the feathers on his chest began to quiver and his wings began to rise and fall until Joy believed that he must be crying. Though the presence of human emotion reassured Joy that her husband, despite his bestial actions, remained in her presence, she found herself in fact wishing that his situation might degrade into that of a mere chicken to save him from suffering so as a half-human.

Joy fetched the wastebin and a bucket of water and cleaned as best she could the stains from the living room carpet, placing the portions of mouse into the wastebin as she worked. Robert, settling himself in front of the fireplace, watched her with what she took to be a contrite expression, and when she had finished cleaning up his mess, he followed her into the kitchen and stood immediately at the doorway, indicating his wish to go out. When she opened the door, he ran straight into the yard and began tearing up the few flowers that had begun to bloom in the ripening spring. When the flowers were hoisted from the soil, Robert started on the grass itself, pulling up small chunks and tossing them aside until he had ruined the entire lawn. Presently he turned on himself, pecking and ripping the small jumper that he had been wearing since the previous day, pulling strand by strand until the thing fell from him and was pushed into the muddy mess by his feet. All the while he screeched and flapped, making more noise than Joy thought possible, jumping up onto the top of their small fence and looking from moment to moment as if he might fall off and onto the other side. Throughout this, Joy could do little but watch her husband's feral tantrum, considering the weight of the guilt that caused him to behave in such a way, and naked too, for Robert had always been a restrained man, not so much as raising his voice in the many years of their marriage. And yet had she not caused this strain, by expecting him to remain human in all the ways she desired? Clothing him and feeding him as if he were a man, and expecting him to hold off the encroaching chicken-ness of his current condition? She waited until the poor Robert-hen ran himself ragged and collapsed by the side of the shed, panting in a way most unbecoming to either chicken or man. After he quieted, she called out to him:

'Robert, come now. You needn't wear clothes anymore, nor eat at the table unless you wish. I will give you nothing but birdseed and the things that you like, and you can hunt as many of those damned mice as you fancy. But you must do one thing for me and keep in the safety of the yard, or even better in the house, for if you continue to cause this commotion a dog will come upon you, or a fox, or even a poacher, and that will be the end of you, and it will be all your own fault.'

But Robert would not come closer, nor into the house, and even when Joy took a pillowcase from the washing line and tried to capture her husband he would not stand still. Instead, he began to peck her calves, and when she gave up her chase and fell back to the end of the garden, Robert fluttered and flapped at the sides of the shed. Of course; he wanted a home of his own, a home that suited his needs more than the cloying cushions of a settee or the suffocating spread of a duvet. He needed a home fit for a hen.

A brief search around Robert's 'everything' drawer in the kitchen unearthed the keys to the rusty padlock, and as soon as the door opened, Robert ran into the musty air of the shed and trod the damp boards to show his pleasure. Here he settled, exploring this nook and that cranny, and in this way it was decided: Robert would live in the shed from then on.

The rest of the day was passed tidying unused garden tools out of the way and sweeping up the remnants of a marriage; broken picture frames, three separate strimmers, all in their boxes, and a long-abandoned rowing machine that Joy had to drag out by the feet. After consulting the internet, Joy brought down large cardboard boxes from the loft, with Robert skittering nervously at the foot of the ladder, and filled them with straw and soft wood shavings that she purchased from the local garden centre – along with a sofa cushion underneath it all, because she couldn't bear the thought of Robert not having any real comfort. She pushed the boxes to the back of the shed where it was darkest, and tidied away some last errant nails and pushpins from the floor, so Robert would not get them stuck in his sinewy feet. Her husband could not contain his delight, flitting from one box to the next, bedding down, flapping the contents around in pleasure and then diving into the next. As the night closed in, Joy closed the door and, opening a window slightly so that Robert might not feel too claustrophobic, padlocked the shed from the outside, for his safety. She fretted as she lay in bed and barely slept, but consoled herself that Robert would be happier, and she would grow used to the separation.

The next morning, soon after sunrise, Joy rushed down to the end of the garden, fraught with worry. But Robert, fresh and happy, had laid not one but two eggs, and happily hopped off his nest to show his wife what he had produced. She took them, thanking him profusely, and fed him his breakfast of seed as she fried up the eggs with a little ham. Now there was little point keeping Robert indoors in the daytime, where he did not want to be, so, leaving the shed door ajar in case he needed some privacy, Joy and Robert took to passing their days outside, and if for some reason Joy had to leave the yard, Robert would retreat back into his shed and allow himself to be locked in, for he had no desire to lose the cosy situation in which he found himself. One early morning in July, Joy was awoken by the sound of a rooster crowing in a field nearby, but she double-checked the padlock on the shed and felt secure that Robert could not get out.

As the summer began, days passed with some short periods of despondency on Joy's part, but otherwise calmly and with little cause for alarm. Robert had his freedom, and Joy, in a manner, had hers. In the afternoons they listened to the radio, Robert pecking here and there, Joy refilling her glass and making her way through a stack of paperbacks, both of them showing affection and respect before they parted for the evening, Joy stumbling a little. On the longest day of the year the couple were in their yard until almost 11 p.m., so fine was the weather and so pleasantly warm the evening, and when Joy went to bed she tripped twice on the stairs and dropped the glass that she was carrying. She woke the next morning in a state of distress, with the sense of unease and embarrassment that one experiences from the age of thirty-five onwards after drinking. It took her several minutes to regain the facts of her situation, and pulling on one of her husband's old shirts she flew down the stairs and out into the garden, only to find her fears confirmed. The shed door remained wide open.

She called out to Robert as she ran and he met her at the entrance; thank the lord, he was still there. But there was something reticent about him, and when she went to collect the morning's egg, Robert would not remove himself from the nest, and indeed pecked at Joy's hand when she tried to shift him. Considering it a sign of his anger for having put him in danger, she left the egg and spent the day apologising profusely, even calling into the radio station to request his favourite composer. Robert's disdain for his wife's error abated as the day went on, yet the next morning he still would not allow his egg to be taken. Nor the day after that, or the day after that. Joy concluded that Robert must have stopped laying altogether, for there would have been a mountain of the things if he was, and she decided to spare him the embarrassment of her morning searches; from now on she would make no enquiries as to the eggs, and if there was one, he would be sure to tell her.

Three weeks later, Joy opened the shed door to find three chicks, freshly hatched, and her husband clucking around them, a proud mother if ever there was one. Look, he seemed to say. Look, dear wife, at what I have made.

Joy dropped to her knees and opened her hands; she had not seen a baby chick since she was a child, when her teacher had allowed them to incubate their own eggs in the classroom. They were tiny and excitable, and as she looked at them and stroked their backs Robert came to her, as he almost never did, and pressed himself to her calf. The morning of the open door, Joy realised – the cockerel must have found his way in, must have found Robert. Must have—

Joy struggled to her feet and almost tripped as she stepped away from the open door. She looked at the foreign creature mothering his brood. Her husband, no doubt – but had Robert not prostituted himself to a beast? Had he not allowed himself into the most savage of acts with a male of the species, submitting to its animal power, and yet where was his shame? Where was his need for forgiveness – from Joy, his wife? The new mother pecked at the scattered fluff of his children, hardly minding that another was there. Her humiliation did not register. She had never felt more alone.

Joy slammed the shed door closed and padlocked it, closing the side window from the outside so nothing might get in. She spent several hours in the kitchen, picking up the phone and putting it down, looking up numbers in the phone book and then tossing it aside, and finally smashing some of their wedding china as the only release she could think of. Taking a bottle with her, Joy retired to the bedroom, though it was still the morning, and she pulled up the summer quilt around her and wept into it until the bottle was empty and she wet the bed, unable to remove herself from her own nest to attend to her basic needs. There, she fell asleep, hiccupping Robert's name and gasping for breath.

After a long sleep, Joy Feather woke resolute. She drew a bath and, refusing to be ashamed of the mess she had made of herself, gently and with no rush washed and perfumed herself, dressing in one of Robert's favourite outfits, a summer dress with neat pumps in a complementary colour. She even pressed her hair and donned a hat, though the weather didn't really call for it. Preparing a tray of various seeds and, having quickly consulted an encyclopaedia, some potato skins rescued from the kitchen bin, she entered the shed to find Robert nestled down with his chicks, which cooed gently upon her entrance. She placed the tray on the straw-covered floor and talked to Robert, tenderly stroking her husband until he hopped onto the floor and helped himself to his breakfast. Joy fancied that there was something different about Robert that morning, that perhaps he had come to the same conclusion that she had. He was quieter than usual and displayed no concern. Yet it was not acceptance she was noticing, it was indifference. Robert, like all new mothers, had cast off the frivolous worries of his previous life and now thought only of his babies, with little regard for the outside world and the people in it – including Joy. After Robert had finished his feed, Joy joined him on the floor and spent a long hour scratching between his feathers and stroking his head while he nuzzled his beak into the soft folds of her stomach. When she eventually produced a folded pillowcase from her pocket her husband barely flinched, and she caught him easily, tossing the chicks into the sack alongside their mother and making her way to the car. When their neighbour Mrs Alderman, who had a reputation as a busybody, leaned over from her own driveway and asked what was in the sack, and where Joy might be going so early in the morning, Joy straightened her back and said, with no hesitation:

'This is Robert, Mrs Alderman, who was turned into a chicken. Surely you must recognise him?'

She opened the pillowcase and thrust it at the woman, at which time Robert began to flap and squawk as if his life depended on it. Trapping him quickly inside, Joy plunged her arm into the bag and grabbed the three chicks in one fist, throwing them onto Mrs Alderman's side of the fence.

'You can give these to the dog, if you've still got her.'

Joy threw the Robert-sack into the back seat of the car and pulled out of the driveway without a single glance at Mrs Alderman. It was a searingly gorgeous day, and Joy took in the blue skies as they drove out of the city and into the countryside. She put on the radio and sang a little; Robert did not join in. It was a forty-five-minute drive to the small farm of their old friend Colin, who they had known since the early days of their marriage, and despite his surprise at their visit, he invited them in immediately for fresh scones and tea. Joy let Robert out of the sack and he pecked nervously around the kitchen as Joy explained the situation. Colin refreshed the teapot twice while she told the tale, and when Joy had finished, there was a long time with only quiet.

'I understand your predicament, Joy, but how will I tell him from the others?'

'You know him well, Colin, just as well as I do, and he has some of the same habits that you know; he is no good at losing, for one, and he enjoys being read to. I think if pushed you would distinguish him with little effort. But for all that, I wonder whether it is necessary for you to tell him from the others. All that matters is that he's amongst his own and in an environment that suits him. Our bare yard just isn't enough to keep a man in the manner to which he's become accustomed. And I can no longer deal with the choices he's made.'

And so it was set. Colin walked the couple out to the small fenced area where two chicken coops were housed, one navy blue and one a bright yellow, and both in good condition. Here twenty-two chickens ran and fussed, and no sooner had Robert seen them than his humanity seemed to slip from him completely; he rushed from Joy and fluttered at the fence gate, clucking to be let in. Colin turned and walked back to the main house as Joy opened the gate, and there was the last moment of it: Robert, now a hen in all regards, stared up at Joy until she got down on her knees and pressed her face to the top of her husband's small feathered head, and there they remained just a second or two before the hen scattered excitedly to find its new brood.

Colin offered Joy a bed for the night and a nip of something stronger than tea, but even when he argued that she'd had quite a shock and could perhaps do with a rest, she waved his suggestions aside, telling him that she would have to get back home and begin looking for a job, for she couldn't subsist on Robert's redundancy pay for all her life and she must alter herself to her present situation. As she drove away, her friend reflected that Joy Feather had gone quite mad, no doubt with the grief of her husband leaving her for a younger woman or some other local tart. Resolving to call on the poor woman more often when he was in the city, he made up a package of pickles and raw butter for posting to her, and every year to mark the anniversary of her visit he sent her a small delivery of fresh meats – the hind legs of a prize pig, a pheasant, a dozen eggs and always two whole chickens.

sixth: tragedies

sadnesses that we know; satisfying pits in which we might wallow,
to think about the facts of our lives and the ways in which they fail us

'TIL DEATH DO US PARTS

Feb 25th 2003. Ms Edie Theadore and the hands of Annabelle Gardner were married by The Rev. Joanne K. Boreland at the Cathedral of St Catherine in Bath.

E die ran the pad of her thumb over her beloved's knuckles. So soft, so supple, so capable, these hands. Breadmaking, brow-stroking, weed-pulling hands. Hands to raise children with. The blood dripped from the severed wrists but everyone gathered was polite enough not to look. They beamed their beatific smiles at the ladyvicar that a friend of Edie's mother had recommended, mouthing *she's one of those, you know.* Edie held the two cold hands in her own, the muscles in her forearms straining slightly with the effort of holding the hands out exactly as if they were still attached to a person – but she kept smiling, kept smiling. Her whole family was there, half under duress but there nonetheless, happy that she was finally settling down after throwing away so many potentials; never quite right, always some small flaw. They had never quite understood that there were so many flaws in Edie that there was no room for any more in her relationships. But now: here was perfection enough to fill up the gaps where Edie was lacking. The ladyvicar asked the question; Edie said her part, then lifted the hands slightly to indicate the corresponding 'I do'. The ladyvicar had been very accommodating in figuring out how exactly the service would go; the main thing was that everyone should see her commit. Smile, smile, smile. It was the happiest day of their lives.

Oct 2nd 2003. Ms Edie Theadore and the right leg of Ms Genevieve Schoof were married by The Rev. Joanne K. Boreland at the Cathedral of St Catherine in Bath.

The church was only half-full this time, but no matter; you couldn't expect everyone to really understand polyamory, nor accept it, and Edie was happy enough that the ladyvicar had agreed to hold the ceremony again. This time, Edie was seated, an almost-empty chair next to her, her beloved's foot in a white slipper on the floor. The calf and knee sprouted upwards, as if a person was growing from the church floor. Edie smiled and put her hand on the inside of the thick, fleshy thigh, a little too brazenly for the middle of their service – but what the hell, would God begrudge them a little pre-emptive consummation? Wedding days were long and exhausting and a spike of excitement would keep them both going. She pinched the gorgeous heft of it between her fingertips. A strong leg; a leg that could squat toddlers and run pushchairs around parks. She couldn't wait to take it home and join it to the rest; you cannot expect to get everything you need from one single person. Instead of a ring, Edie placed a ribbon around the ankle of her beloved and hoped it didn't look too much like she had been tagged. She carried the leg out in her arms and people threw rice as they left the church.

September 1st 2004. Ms Edie Theadore and the pelvis of May Stephanie Masterson were married by The Rev. Reginald Gilbert at the Cathedral of St Catherine in Bath.

The organ echoed. Edie stood at the front of the church with a nephew at her side. The boy held up a red silk pillow on which lay the hips of her beloved. The ladyvicar had been moved on at the end of her tenure, and the man in her place seemed uncomfortable with the whole situation. Edie was not, however; Edie was glowing with quiet bliss. She gently fingered the trim of the pillow, holding herself back from taking the bones in her hands and licking them all over. A slight clack of nail on calcium was enough consent for the listless reverend; when it was Edie's turn, she took the pillow from the nephew, said 'I do', and tenderly pressed her hand to the pelvis. A little matter remained on the bones but it would wear away, in time. They were child-bearing hips, as her mother, God rest her soul, might have said. Hips with sway and sass and purpose; hips that would take a woman where she wanted to go. The rice clattered on the pelvis like rainfall as they left.

June 27th 2005. Ms Edie Theadore and the two earlobes of Emma Constance Blair were married by The Rev. Stephen Moore at the Cathedral of St Catherine in Bath.

A Tuesday afternoon, to accommodate no one but themselves, and two small pieces of skin in a ring box; Edie held them out as if showing them off and the vicar spoke directly to them, his cheeks a deep red as he did so. The choir, dressed in white and crimson, strained to look as Edie read out the vows once, twice; a glance from the vicar put their bums back on seats. It was a brief ceremony, what with Edie being very keen to get them both back home to the rest of their little family. She imagined taking one between her lips as it lay on the pillow, the sweat of the night-time dissolving on her tongue. Pure, soft, unpierced; they were perfect, these earlobes, just like the leg had been perfect, and the hands, and the hips, and the other parts she'd collected. She broke out in goosebumps at the thought of them all at home waiting for her; the vicar saw the shiver and raised an eyebrow. But nothing would ruin their special day, not even the disdain of a man of the cloth. Service over, Edie snapped the ring box closed and slipped it into her pocket. She walked straight home from the church.

September 5th 2010. Ms Edie Theadore and the lips of Hannah Moore were married by The Rev. Alexander Regis at the Cathedral of St Catherine in Bath.

THIS IS MY BODY, GIVEN FOR YOU

It was just Edie, the lips and the vicar. Family and friends had long since disowned her, and the parish had decided that this would be the last marriage that Edie was allowed to have – in their jurisdiction, at least. Edie had fought them on principle but, truth be told, her project was almost finished. These lips were the final pieces of a particular puzzle. It had taken years to find the right ones and now here they were, resting in the palm of her hand, a little flaccid from the lack of blood but not much could be done about that. There were collagen injections and fillers and all sorts of things available, but not until after, not until they were legally wed. Until then, these lips did not belong to her, and the rest of her beloved would have to learn patience. The vicar did not wait to hear a second 'I do'; he garbled his part and closed the book, turning his back on Edie before she'd even finished. He seemed disgusted with himself for his role in it, and Edie pitied him; how sad to be so behind the times. He couldn't even see the beauty in her bride. No matter; Edie kissed the lips in her hand and left, satisfied.

She could not wait until the evening; it was late afternoon when Edie took the now-rusting needle and stitched the perfect, plump lips of Hannah Moore onto the face of Rita Eckhart, underneath the hair of Lorraine Price, on the skull of Patricia Cleeve-Morton, on the neck of Lee-Lee Pascale, on the shoulders of Stevie Cox, from which protruded the left arm of Lucy Bloom and the right arm of Jennie Fitzcohen, both of which ended in the hands of Annabelle Gardner, parenthesising the breasts and torso of Valeria de Diego, on the hips of May Stephanie Masterson, from which extended the left leg of Ann Parr and the right leg of Genevieve Schoof, completed by the glorious, most ideal feet of Hayley Stewart. So many faultless parts all fitted and sewn and glued in place. Edie could not wait; she carried her perfect bride, put together so thoughtfully and with such precision, through to the marital bed, the bed that had been waiting so many years to feel the weight of two complete people coming together as one.

Two full bodies intertwined; one mouth running along clammy cold skin, adoring every part. Edie whispered to her perfect bride, spread her legs, took a nipple in her mouth. Edie flinched, pulled away, then wiped the thin trickle of blood from where the harsh stitches around the areola had cut her. She tried again, sucked on those heavenly fingers, dug her nails into the fleshy hips. But the skin did not respond. Her bride was silent. Truth be told, a damp sickness was growing in the pit of Edie's stomach; she had expected the tummy flip, the overwhelming love, the itch of effortless desire, but there was nothing.

But was there ever, on the wedding night? Really?

Edie retched as her mouth ran over the dead, empty parts. She nibbled at the lifeless patchwork ragdoll in her arms. She hummed a little to keep from crying, and kept the smile on her face. It must be perfect. It should be perfect. The happiest day of their lives.

COO

At the three-month scan they give you the basic uterus guard. Polycarbonate sheets and stretchy sides. It goes all the way under and up at the back, and rubs on the softest part of your inner thighs. At the six-month scan it's made of Kevlar and adjusts to fit your growing bump. Six straps and a protective foam comfort layer. It cuts you between your legs and you'll bleed. Before three months it's just hands over the belly – although really, she doesn't bother with the three-monthers at all since most of them go away anyway.

She comes nearest your due date, to make it hurt the most. You've seen her a million times, in your dreams and in stories and in textbooks and pamphlets, but still you'll pin an artist's impression of her onto your fridge as you slip into your third trimester and start the real round of worrying. Her face just above the egg tray in the fridge, so there's no chance you'll forget what you're looking for.

Two months left and you'll stop going out. Four weeks and it's next of kin only allowed in the house. A week 'til the birth and you'll lock your bedroom door from the inside. But there's no matter. She gets in. She gets busy. Not a single baby born in a decade.

You'll shutter your windows and check the wardrobe for feathers. You'll look under the bed and close the bathroom and run from the switch to the bed when you turn the lights off at night. You'll pull the sheets up to your chin and pray to a god you don't believe in to deliver your baby safely.

But you'll hear the scrape-scrape of her claws down the walls of the house at 2 a.m. on a Thursday. You'll see the shadows cast in the window by her wings. When her monstrous bill smashes through the double glazing, you'll throw the covers back, weeping, because the body next to you cannot help you now and you might as well get on with your grieving.

Everyone knows the story these days. It is whispered in prenatal clinics, at coffee mornings, in the changing rooms at the gym. The details are always the same: a woman, Leda, gave birth to a child. The child came out *en caul* and the nurses fluttered around it; so rare, for a baby to be born in its amnion, the two layers of the sac so perfectly intact. They cooed and lifted the baby for the mother to see; it's lucky, they said, she'll be safe from drowning. But to burst the thing they had to crack it; the membranes were thicker, more solid than they should have been. The nurses gasped as the child unfurled into life: partially shrouded in grey-white fur and half-blind, a silent little sack of wet skin with arms folded in, all thin legs and distended belly and long nose. As they stepped away from the medical table the mother saw, and muttered *Christ Almighty*, and then *It looks just like its father*. They tried to put it in her arms, but she hugged herself and refused to take it, so they placed the ragged thing in an old incubator, thinking it might die.

But it did not die. It shed its fur and plumage burst forth; it opened its eyes and its nose hardened into a glorious bill. It gained weight and wingspan. Its fingers stretched out from between its feathers. By three weeks it was plump and it stood on its skinny legs, clattering its bill at the doctors and patients, so they wrapped it in a towel and forced the mother to take it home.

The mother placed her bird-baby in the cot she'd built for it. It shat on the pink sheets and ripped cotton from the mattress with its talons. As Leda looked down on the blackening wing tips and reddening legs, she said, *On the papers they wrote Helen, but I will call you Coo.*

Leda fed the baby small frogs and goldfish from the pet shop, but she could not stand to touch the child and had nightmares about her conception. As soon as the bird-baby could fly on her own, Leda opened a window and pushed her out. After several days screeching outside her mother's locked front door, Coo nested in the roof of a nearby church, scrabbling into a hole in the ceiling and making a bed for herself with paper and straw. It was warm, and there were songs from the choir. She was settled and safe – until a week later, in the middle of Sunday service, when part of the ceiling fell in and the congregation all saw her.

At first, they were curious, jostling to see what it was that had made its home in the rafters. But soon someone fetched a ladder and in the light of their torches she was hideous, with her white-grey excrement clinging to her underside and the patches of pink baldness where she'd pulled her feathers out with stress. They took the ladders and trapped her in with broken boards from the street, hoping she might die. But she did not die; she stayed in her closed space, too scared to escape. They grew to hate the smell of her shit, the sound of her clattering, the scratching at the ceiling in the middle of the sermon. In the night-times teenage boys brought ladders and climbed up to her, burning her with cigarettes and putting bands around her bill. They bothered her, and abused her, and would not even step aside to let her escape. The bird-girl was trapped. She buried her head in her wings and rattled her bill at all hours. She started to lay, four eggs at a time, settling her warm body on top of each one to pray for it to hatch. She would create something of her own; something that did not hate her.

It was the women who noticed. Peering through the hole while the vicar droned on, they saw her worried fluttering and heard her soft cooing. Climbing into the ceiling, they peered under her filthy girth and shit-matted feathers to see shell smooth as river rock. They thought of what those eggs would become, and they came closer, hands open, all smiles.

No place for babies, they said, grinning. *Let us take them. Let us warm them 'til they hatch, then wash off the shell.*

She unfolded herself from the nest, and on tall legs stepped uneasily aside. The women held her. She wept into them, a squawking sob that cut their ears. Their arms tightened around her. The women took the eggs in blankets, performatively gentle, admiring the strength of protective shells. Coo began to clatter, but they held her.

They passed the eggs down and out of the hole, then climbed down the ladder, leaving Coo alone. The men took the eggs in their hands and began to throw and catch them; Coo dropped down out of her hole, panicking, and the men scurried away, putting their hoods up against her talons and laughing as they screamed their plans: *a fucking big omelette.*

You'll pay for that sin, now. You'll pay like the rest of them. The stork-woman stands on her skinny, long legs and she smells the potential of babies like hers. She soars over the town sniffing out a ripe foetus, waiting for the moment to cause the most pain.

When the time is right, you'll know her stench, the astringent smell of the bleach she now uses to keep herself clean, and as you faint into unconsciousness you'll feel the sharp scratch at the straining part of your stomach, or feel the cold, alien bill, wet from the marshlands, begin its slow and awful journey up inside you. You will tense your thighs, but as you faint with the pain it will force you open. Coming for the baby. Coming for the baby.

You wake in a sweat as your due date crawls closer. You won't wait like the others. You've decided to stop this. With your hand on your stomach you take your mother's marble rolling pin from behind the kitchen drawer and creep up to your bedroom, listening for her noise.

You'll think of the smaller birds in your freezer; the chicken, the duck, the turkey, the pheasant. You'll think of meat inside meat, stuffing, the bread sauce and the mess of it. You'll think of the push and the struggle and the work to get it all inside. The strain of it when it feels like nothing will go. You'll stuff her and brine her and roast her and carve, letting the men take the fat parts, letting the children have the legs.

You'll listen for the scrape–scrape of her claws down the walls of the house. You'll let your hand fall to the side of the bed as you see the shadows cast in the window by her wings. When her bill, that cold bill, smashes through the double glazing, you'll throw the covers back, laughing, raising the pin in your hand, lifting it up, stretching the muscles that hold your child, because the body inside you makes you wild.

WET LIKE JELLY

It's strange looking into your son's eyes when they're staring back at you from inside some other kid's face. Uncanny. I could feel the cold sting of regret nip at my Achilles, truth be told, but there was no going back now. He was my responsibility.

'D'ya want a biscuit?' I asked the lad.

'No,' he said, pointing Dylan's pupils at the floor. I got the Rich Teas out of the cupboard anyway and put them next to his cup. Dylan would probably have wanted a biscuit. His mam always had a sweet tooth.

'No!', he yelled, sending a cloud of crumbs flying into my face. I counted three and breathed out through my mouth slowly, wiping the mess from my lips. Weekends away, they were never easy. Once we got some food in us, we'd be more settled. Hunger does no one any favours.

I opened the fridge but there was nothing edible in there, only a pint of semi-skimmed that might have been there since the millennium, going by the smell. My fault, really. I should have stopped on the drive up and got some basics. The place was hardly kid-friendly either. Not really a great start to this whole father–son thing. Still, we'd make it work.

We'd have to. I said as much to the lad and he looked up at me with tears in Dylan's eyes and I damn near started crying right there and then.

They said it was a miracle of medical science that we could take our son's eyes out of his body and put them straight into another little baby. I asked why such a miracle couldn't have brought our kid back to life when he died for no reason inside my wife's belly at 40 weeks, but the doctor just looked at his feet and my wife turned away and said, 'Alan don't', as if it wasn't a bit hypocritical to be talking about miracles at a time like that. Three days later she was still in that ward, getting prodded and poked and smeared and whatnot, and the doctor thought it was a good idea to bring me the kid's fucking eyes, in some sort of medical container all covered in tubes and mechanics, as if to prove what a fucking miracle worker he was. They were blue, so light they were almost grey, just like my dad's, and they were so wet and like jelly that I wouldn't have been surprised if they'd looked right up at me. He held them out to me, but I couldn't take the box.

'Alan don't', she said again when I started to tell that doctor that he'd ruined my little lad and he'd never be right again, and I'll be damned if a minute later she didn't have hold of that box like it was the boy himself. She'd have put it right to her breast if it had a mouth. Sick started coming up in me and when I got outside I couldn't even light a fag, my hands were shaking so much. The box was gone when I got back upstairs.

'D'ya need a piss?' I asked the lad, wary that we'd come a long way and he might go down his legs and onto the kitchen chair. He said no and I asked him again, because sometimes they need prodding a bit, these kiddies, that's what my sister says at least and she's got five of them. He still said no, and looked a bit bored, and I was trying to keep him on good terms so I let it go. He kicked his feet against the table, spilling my drink and his, creating a lake of watery tea beneath the mugs. He was definitely bored.

'So, what do you – you know… do? Usually?'

'What?'

'What do you do? When you're at home?'

'I don't know.'

'Well come on lad, you must have some idea.'

'I do Lego. Read books. Help Mum with the baby. I don't know.'

I looked at the musty rooms around us, the empty living room open to the kitchen. Nothing in here, nothing in there. The rest, a bust.

'So… telly?'

He sat himself on the sofa, releasing a breath of old decades from the material, and after a bit of tinkering I managed to get the Sky box on, flicked to some animated rubbish, feeling some sense of achievement. Then someone said fuck and I realised it was too late in the day for Scooby Doo.

'Wait. Are you allowed to watch these?'

He ignored me, engrossed in the too-adult figures in front of him. I tried to sift through my head for rules and guide-lines. Nothing.

'Are you sure you don't need a piss?'

He screamed in the negative, turning up the volume on his cartoons, so I found a can of warm lager from the cupboard and had myself a bit of a think.

Next time I looked over, there was a growing patch of piss on the crotch of his shorts. I grabbed him under the arms and ran him upstairs, kicked open the bathroom door and plonked him in front of the loo. He didn't move, and the darkness grew bigger.

'Can't you pull your pants down?' I ran through vague memories of dads in petrol station toilets, trying to remember whether they went in with their kids, and whether it was just the little ones that needed a hand, but – how little? How can you tell their age?

'It's not that!' The sob in it cut through me.

'Haven't you been… trained?'

'Shut the door, shut the door!'

He clutched his wet crotch and screamed the words, and when I slammed the bathroom door from the inside he only screeched louder. Outside, I listened for the trickle. Caught nothing. With five minutes gone I started to panic, thinking of heads down toilets and drownings in an inch of bath water and I kicked the locked door in, thinking him dead, but instead found him desperately weeping, wet clothes on the floor, him trying to wrap a dusty beige towel around his privates as if it was a nappy.

We had no spares, of course. Nothing in any of the wardrobes neither. Eventually I let him dry off his bits, put his pants and shorts on the back of a radiator and got him leg by leg into a used but dry pair of my old boxers that I found in my football bag in the back of the car. I looked the place over for a safety pin to no avail, so he had to make do with a clothes peg to keep them up. If he hadn't been shaking quite so much, I might just have laughed.

I could prove myself a bit with dinner, I thought, but accidentally chucked the jar of sauce on the floor, spilling most of it, sending shards of glass scuttling everywhere under his tender little feet. He cried a bit while I was cooking the pasta, proper crying too, biting his bottom lip and wailing with his mouth shut, and it made my hands shake because I'd never seen any of my kids crying. I thought I might faint and that he'd get away, but he stopped after a while and came and sat at the table to eat, yawning like it was well past his bedtime. I offered him a bit of lager but he said no, so he had weak tea with no milk and for afters we had a tin of peaches with some squirty cream that had gone out of date. By turns he looked dead scared and dead tired, and I realised I hadn't had cause to make conversation with a six-year-old since I was a lad myself.

'What time's your bedtime?'

'Half seven. I mean – nine,' he said, eyes widening. Let him have it, I thought. It's half eleven anyway. Cheeky little sod.

I looked all over for entertainment and found a pack of cards, just 49 as it turns out, but I figured it didn't really matter, not for a little one. We tried poker with pennies for chips, then gin rummy, then twist, but it was all beyond him bar snap – that tedium – and after a couple of games he started kicking my shins and saying he was bored. So telly it was, again, an action film with guns and titties; damaging, no doubt, but at least it filled the long hour 'til he looked tired enough to sleep.

'Do you need a story?'

'I'm not a baby, you know. I'm in the Cubs. I've been camping in the woods and everything.'

'It's not only babies need stories, my lad.'

'I haven't got my toothbrush. My mouth's dirty. You're bad at this.'

'Ni' mind son, them's only your baby ones. They'll all fall out regardless, brush or no brush.'

He looked on the verge of tears again, which I didn't get, really, as it wasn't exactly a cruel thing to say, but seeing as how I was a couple of cans in and the upset had already started to subside, I had the urge to comfort him a bit.

'Look, we won't be here long at all, alright kidda? There's some Polo mints in the car if your mouth tastes like shite and you'll likely be home in a couple of mornings anyway.'

He was quieter after. The wind out of him. Washed his face without prompting, because I'd no idea to tell him, then got himself a blanket out of the cupboard. I hadn't realised it was cold. He was out like a light and I had a bit of a moment then, not just the guilt, the regret, but realising how I'd never seen my lad's eyes flicker shut at night, never seen them trying to fight off tiredness. When my lad came out his eyes were fused shut, just like all the ones before him. With normal dead babies you've to pry their eyelids open with a wet cotton bud so you can pretend that your baby's blinking and that they can have a nice look at their dadda. I didn't have any time to work on them eyes, though, not Dylan's. The next time I saw them they were in a fucking box in some doctor's hands, without any lids or lashes or sockets around them.

They asked us about the eyes just after they'd said he was dead. We'd said no on all the donor forms like usual and I thought it was a bit of a shit move, really, to ask that of a woman who'd just been told that another little 'un was going to come out of her dead and that she might as well stop trying. My wife leaned over her belly and signed the form before I'd even had a chance to say no. The doctor banged on about the transplant being a worldwide first as if that meant it wouldn't be so bad to drive home with an empty car seat again and have to tell all the neighbours that no, that massive bump stuck to the front of my wife for near on ten months hadn't ended up being anything good, and I couldn't even breathe for the thought that I wouldn't get that little body this time, I couldn't even protest, let alone rip up that form and tell that doctor to go fuck himself because we'd made them eyes. They were ours. I was paralysed with the thought of his little head with nothing in it.

She seemed alright, that was the worst of it. Once her insides were gone it was like she'd got a second wind, telling everybody that her baby was the baby whose eyes they'd taken out whole, first proper eye transplant an' all that, as if it was an achievement to have had one die. She kept all the paper cuttings in a little album and I had to say love, this is getting a bit much, don't you think, and she said you better fuck off Alan because this is all I've got now, this is all people will remember of any of those kids. Because of this, my lad's life had a purpose. You've got your horrible little garden and I've got this so you keep your mouth shut and I won't tell anyone about your project out there. And I thought, you wouldn't dare, you stupid cow, but I didn't say it, and it's when you don't say it that things start to go bad, isn't it? So a year later she'd moved back in with her mam and a year after that we were signing divorce papers and a year after that I'd lost my job, and they said it was just layoffs, more cuts Alan, though we all knew it was because I came to work with fag ends in my hair and breath that was 40 percent proof.

I watched some more telly with another couple of cans. All gambling phone-in shows and reruns of programs that were shit twenty years ago, but it was a good bit of noise to drown out the crying. A constant wail, I couldn't stop it, the sound only cutting out when I took another sip of beer. Bad at this, I thought, and it was right, and I begged then, in my head at least, for them to hurry up and get here. I wanted done with it. I wanted it over, couldn't do it. Failure. I wanted rescue.

The only thing that calmed me was the realisation that they must already be halfway here.

The woman at the transplant centre had probably let the police know that I'd been there asking questions, as I'd had a bit of a breakdown in the foyer and she had to have security put me back in my car. A green Nissan Micra with a busted rear window wouldn't be that hard to find, and we'd had to stop for a piss and a packet of crisps more than once on the way up so we must have been seen. If they'd got into my flat and found Isaac and Emma and Tess and all the other kids buried in the garden then they'd be after me like a mad dog after a rabbit anyway. It's not illegal to bury them in a garden – I'd checked – but the house was only rented and they were only very shallow graves, dug dozens of times because sometimes, increasingly often these days, I just needed to put my hands on the wood, to be close to them, my little lost children. Seven little kids all perfectly formed and only our Dylan without his fucking eyes. The police would dig them up one last time, and probably open them as well to check I hadn't interfered with them, and then in Dylan's body they'd find the glass eyes I put in to try and make him whole again, and they'd come for me like I was the bloody Moors murderer. Strange, they'd say. He must be after that little boy, a bad man. They'd ask no questions, they wouldn't try to understand. Just a few more hours, then, fingers crossed.

I wondered if the kid might have to get up in the night to have a cry or a piss or whatever, but when I looked in it was near on three and he was still dead to the world. Mouthy little shite, really. I touched his blonde hair and watched his shoulders go up and down every time he took in a breath. Dylan wouldn't have been mouthy. Dylan wouldn't have been blonde. His mam's grandma was from Trinidad and our family's all mousey brown, so Dylan would have had dark hair, a full head of it. You could see a bit of it when he came out, though it was all stuck to his skull and there wasn't much of it anyway, and these days he was bald as a cue ball. Dark hair and blue eyes; he would have been a killer, our Dylan. A mild-mannered lady-killer, never talking back to his dad or pissing in his pants or making it hard to raise him.

I'd had it in my head that this lad would have had thick dark hair too, so when I got a look at him in the playground with all that yellow hair, I thought I'd got the wrong kid. It was alright once I finally got hold of him and put him in the car. He was just quiet really, and so was I, but when we got on the M1 I started to think about what I'd done and I went a bit loopy if I'm honest, talking to the lad and saying it's alright Dylan we're not going far Dylan we're just going to have a little holiday Dylan. The lad started weeping and I had to lock him in the car for a bit and leave it on the hard shoulder and have a wander until I gathered myself back up again.

I found some dusty gin at the back of the pantry as it was getting light and poured it all into a pint glass. I'd decided by then; if there was no sign of them by noon, I'd drive us both in. Put this whole thing to bed. Get the fucking thing over with. I couldn't imagine what I'd been thinking in the first place, couldn't remember the thought process that had led me to that spot, with some kid that I'd never known, playing a role I didn't know how to play.

The lad came down about half six, wiping sleep out of Dylan's eyes and asking if he could have a glass of water, so I got him one and put some of last night's pasta in a bowl. He sat across from me, spilling sauce into the table, knocking water on the floor, and I thought he's a stranger, this lad. Someone else's little boy. A little troublemaker, really. Dylan would have been a good 'un, although me and his mam wouldn't have been all that good at bringing him up. We'd never had the practice. Never had the patience. Not even with each other, really. Too much anger and not enough love. Probably for the best, really. I probably would have had to give up all their bodies if he'd lived. It's a bit maudlin and all that, having dead kids near where your live kid sleeps, and I wasn't really ready to say goodbye to all them kids yet. My real kids. Good sleepers, always close, no bother at all.

I drained the gin. Watched the kid finish his pasta. Then, as it was all getting fuzzy and I could hear all the sirens coming through the woods, I grabbed the lad and kissed his eyes and held him and let my tears fall onto his blonde hair.

seventh: love stories

    for there has to be some light in the world, even when there is none, and love stories are how we look for it, but it strikes me that the term is ill-defined, because love is all things, both dark and light, both positive and negative, and does a love story just mean a story about the love one person has for another, or can it be a story about the love a man has for his goat, or for the process of cheese-making, or his bloodied fists when he has pummelled someone's head into the ground? is it love to become that goat, that cheese, that mess of puddled brain? it is dangerous not to think of necessary and sufficient conditions when you choose these terms, for such phrases can cover all manner of sins, and allow actions into the world when they should be rejected, and it might cover them over with excuses, and amidst all of this readers might be caught unawares and left feeling quite worse than they did before they began reading

HUMAN MUMMY CONFECTION

Eligible Bachelor Trait 1:
Opens doors for others

You were studying classics, which I considered a frivolous use of ten thousand pounds, and you were brought up Catholic, which excited me because all the lapsed Catholics I knew were total perverts. I knew these things because I'd asked someone about you, someone you'd had a brief dalliance with several months before. They said you had a bit of a hero complex, being the oldest of four and obscenely handsome, but that you had strong thighs and a willingness to humiliate yourself for the pleasure of others. You cried slightly too earnestly at a stage version of *The Elephant Man* and were prone to using terms like 'dalliance'. You appeared to like women too, as I watched you flirt with several freshers across the union bar one night, but after an hour you grew bored of them and gravitated back to the men. You were the subject of my fantasies for a few weeks before we made contact; you held the door open for me and kept holding it for the length of time it took me to get my wheelchair through – unlike most people, who hand the responsibility off to the nearest stranger after thirty seconds. I said *thanks* and you said *no worries* and I, with characteristic confidence, said *so, drink after class then?* and you smiled and said *sure.*

Eligible Bachelor Trait 2: Takes pride in the way he looks

You were tender, and giving, and happy to receive; you were patient with my mobility and listened to the list of things you could not do to me, lest my bones break or the blood pool under my skin at a heavy touch. You let me take the lead and afterwards you checked me for any signs you might have damaged me in the throes of it; a few cuts and my back ached, but that was me on a good day. You had three tattoos in Hanzi; I chose to ignore them. I thought we might be a one-time thing, but the next day after class you were lingering at the place we'd met, sucking on a bar of Kendal Mint Cake, and insisted on walking me to my next seminar, though it was all the way across campus and would have made you late for next period. You did not push me, instead walking beside me and speaking in excessively loud tones and unnecessary details about the previous evening. You arrived unannounced that night with flowers and ran me a bath. You helped me in, read poetry to me from the toilet seat (lid down) and exfoliated my face with a mixture of baking soda and honey, which closes the pores and keeps you young, apparently. You started to massage my feet and when I hid them underneath the water, gently saying it would cause a bruise, you looked so guilty you might have cried. I told you it was fine, that I wasn't made of paper, that I just had to be more careful than others. Just your run-of-the-mill brittle bone disorder. Later we played *Bomberman* to your obvious disdain and I made something Indonesian, which you declared the best thing you'd eaten in years even though you only drank the broth and left all the vegetables. In bed you placed yourself beneath me not one time but three. Afterwards you put a face mask on me, as semen, you told me, is drying.

Eligible Bachelor Trait 3:
Has fantastic communication skills.

The first time you said 'boyfriend' we were at the pub with your classmates, who'd all come from private school and saw me as some sort of interesting folly, the sort of thing you might keep on the edge of the grounds in a small house and show off to the neighbours when they came to visit; look, darling, isn't he quite so different. You'd stopped drinking your very occasional gin and tonic, considering alcohol an assault on the body, but as the rest of them grew more tawdry they leaned in to ask me about maintenance grants and sharing the bathwater and you, gently, pushed them back; *be careful with my boyfriend, will you, he bruises easy.* I was ready to scrap the whole thing, to kiss you goodnight and goodbye after the torture of their company was over, but you let the word so easily slide out of your mouth that it pulled me back in, made me ignore the condescending nature of the sentence as a whole. We got a cab home on your credit card and you got on your knees in the stairway, ignoring my entreaties to get inside before someone saw us. You changed your social media status before we slept, and took me out for breakfast at the fancy gluten-free place, the place I'd have previously said was full of twats, and read to me from Baudelaire, which I found tedious at best. You ate nothing, drinking only cup after cup of hot water and lemon, adding honey in amounts that made my teeth ache at the sight of it.

Eligible Bachelor Trait 4: Is not afraid of his spiritual side

You moved in bit by bit and with no announcement. You had few possessions and what I thought was an overnight bag was in fact your entire wardrobe, library and assortment of knick-knacks. Your ex-flatmate told me he'd been instructed to throw everything else away when you had stopped paying rent several months before. When I tried to talk to you about it, you claimed that it was to make my life easier and that I ought to appreciate the help, given my situation. Soon you were waking up at the crack of dawn to clean the pristine flat and lay my clothes out on the end of the bed, having ironed them and hung them from the radiator so they would be warm when I put them on. You served me a cooked breakfast every morning, stuffed a packed lunch in my backpack and if you didn't cook in the evening you took me out for dinner, making a big deal about accessibility when you phoned to make the reservation. You were warm and comfortable when we got into bed at night and the attention was flattering and

THIS IS MY BODY, GIVEN FOR YOU

patronising in equal measure, so I didn't mention the strange
sweet smell in the bathroom, or the fact that you tasted odd
during sex. It was a letter from the university that alerted
me to the fact that you'd given up your course, and when I
tried to talk to you about it you said that I should really try
yoga, waxing lyrical about how it had sorted out your bad
hip alignment and the wonders it might make for my 'condition'. I slammed the door as I left but you were meditating when I got back, chanting obnoxiously and stinking the
place out with cheap incense. I played The Cure but you still
murmured on. I kicked you over but you did not respond;
you just lay on your back letting the guttural whining grow
louder and louder. When I went to the kitchen to find the
Scotch I realised you'd taken over a cupboard and filled it
with one thing only.

Eligible Bachelor Trait 5:
Displays consistency

Your first excuse was a sore throat, and you brushed off the
suggestion that gargling with salt water would be better
for you. Your second excuse was that you needed to gain
weight and it was heavy in calories, being almost pure sugar.
There was no third excuse, for every time I brought up
the empty jars in the recycling you just stuck your head
in your well-worn copy of a Chinese medical book from
the sixteenth century or, worse, started meditating again.
You drank cups of it morning, noon and night, sometimes
mixed with warm water, sometimes not. You stopped seeing

your arsehole friends and wouldn't come out with mine. I wanted to call your family but didn't know if they even existed. If you weren't running around after me, listless and clearly weak yet stubbornly dedicated to completing tasks I could have easily done myself, you were in the lotus position on the bedroom floor. We stopped having sex the day I came home early and found you hunched over the toilet, golden shit running from you like treacle, you clutching your stomach and moaning (or was it chanting?) in agony. I called an ambulance; you wouldn't get in. *Alexander the Great's sarcophagus was filled with it*, you said, and I refrained from mentioning that he also named a city after his favourite fucking horse.

Eligible Bachelor Trait 6: Is not afraid of commitment

I tried to move out but came back after a day, terrified for you, and found you semi-conscious on the carpet, still sitting, still making noise, having reached an apparent state of semi-divinity, or at least according to passages you'd highlighted in one of your books. You came back down to earth when you heard me talking to the mental health ward, and crawled, molasses-like, to unplug the phone from the wall. I held your face and called you an idiot; there were crystals at the corners of your eyes and you stank, but still you were smiling. Over the next two days we didn't move from the bed, me holding you and trying to force you to sip hot tea, or lick a spoonful of Marmite, and you babbled on, mostly incoherent, about how everyone could eat you, later, take bits of your body and consume them and get all the goodness out of you. You grinned throughout. In a rare moment of clarity you told me it was all for me, poor me, poor delicate me. *I'll heal you*, you said, and I said *I'm fine, you narcissistic motherfucker.*

Eligible Bachelor Trait 7:
Will die for you

You fell asleep and I could take it no longer; you had started to violently purge by the time the ambulance finally came. As they entered the flat they approached me, confused, but I pointed to you, saying *not me, for fuck's sake, it's him, the one covered in his own bile.* You told the nurse at the hospital, in the short periods of respite from your endless throat singing, that you wanted your casket to be filled with it. That night you fell into a coma and no amount of stomach pumping could bring you back. Your corpse smelled like spun sugar. The nurse told your parents what you'd said and like fools they concurred. The process cost a fortune; they used manuka straight from New Zealand and, as per your scrawled will, put you in the ground with a copy of the *Bencao Gangmu* and a portrait of Alexander the Great. As the others drank hot toddies at the wake, I lit a small fire and burned the letter you'd left for me, telling me to dig you up in a decade and eat your sweet, sweet remains and think of how much you loved me.

A MEAL FOR THE
MAN IN TAILS

In Taoism, it is believed that a wake should last seven days and be held in the home. On the final night of the wake, the family of the deceased put out food for the deities that will escort the deceased's soul through the netherworld and into the beyond. The family often put out a delicate fish for the deity to eat, hoping that the difficulty of picking the meat from the bones will give them more time with the departing soul of their loved one.

MENU

amuse-bouche
braised kohlrabi with roasted garlic and truffle oil

The table is set for one. She places the cold dish on top of the slate and adjusts the cutlery beside it. It has been a long time since she's laid the settings herself, now having staff to do it for her. In the kitchen, behind her, things sizzle and steam, different courses prepped and pre-cooked and ready for coming together. She tries not to think of the tiny box in the next room, the box that has been there for seven days now. She wipes her hands on her unwashed chef's jacket and tries to quiet her trembling. Last time the man had come, she had not been expecting him. This time, she is prepared.

He does not knock. He pushes open the door and sweeps in, the tails of his dress coat swimming in his stead. His waistcoat is expensively tailored, pulling him in at all the right places, sitting flat against him. His trousers have the perfect crease. His cufflinks are solid silver. His tie is tastefully colourless, twisted and turned into a half-Windsor, and above it there is no face, no eyes, just a mouth and a nose. The man gently closes the door and takes his seat at the table, brushing his tails out from under him.

As if called, a baby girl crawls in from the next room. She is painted in watercolours, the carpet faintly visible beneath her, just as her father was when he emerged from his box to meet his chauffeur. The baby girl seats herself in the middle of the dining room floor to wait.

salad
marinated beetroot with goat's cheese

She takes a crisp white, fruity not tart, from the fridge and twists out the cork. She flinches as her biceps brush against her swollen breast, the inflamed tissue sensitive through her shirt. She carefully fills his wine glass as he slices what's in front of him with practiced delicacy. The constituent parts of the dish are spread as far away from each other as they can be, so he has to slice the beetroot, and get it on his fork, then slice the cheese, and get it on the fork, to eat each nuanced mouthful. With good manners, each bite takes just that little bit too long. She smiles. She must play the game for a while longer, must make him comfortable, must make him briefly forget his charge. She keeps herself from looking at her child, on the floor, sitting upright. Baby girl always had a strong back.

Hospitality; pure hospitality and nothing more. She is Michelin-starred and she is merely extending a professional hand to her guest, a person that comes by as part of his work. The child on the floor between them is incidental. When the meal is over, the man will take her baby, her watercolour baby, away from the living world and on to the place she will reside. The meal is simply a courtesy. That is what she wants him to believe.

She lets him sit for a few minutes when he has finished. His vague odour of wet soil and rot intrudes as she takes the neatly emptied plate in front of him.

appetiser:
steamed asparagus, hollandaise and boiled egg

He nods as she presents the food, a small tilt of the head to acknowledge the precise and tender nature of the dish. The egg sliced impossibly thin, the sauce neither cloying nor watery, the asparagus beneath it all fresh green and bright as day.

He eats so smartly, so slowly, his movements considered. She has seen it before, in the manner of the funeral directors that dealt with her husband. Unobtrusive, inoffensive, mindful of the fact that though your presence may be necessary, nobody wants you there. She recalls that tomorrow those same men will return for her daughter's body. She puts the thought far from her mind.

She looks over his shoulder at the girl. The baby seems to have grown since her death, seems to have filled out in the cheeks and in her creased thighs, though it may just be that the outlines of her are less distinct than they were before.

seafood:
flash-fried octopus with fennel and orange

The plate is overloaded. The octopus is overcooked. It took all her effort to watch it fry in the pan for two, three, four minutes longer than she should have allowed, but it pays off when she watches his jaw struggling with the rubbery flesh, masticating it into something more edible, giving her more time, more precious time.

As he chews, she steps backwards, just out of his sight, and turns towards the shape of the child. Her body aches to feed the baby. She lowers herself and extends her hand, though she knows that there is nothing to touch. Nothing physical. Last time the man with no eyes came, she reached out to touch her husband and her palm slid right through him. But she reaches out regardless, and again finds nothing there that is real.

THIS IS MY BODY, GIVEN FOR YOU

fish:

beer-battered mackerel with English mustard, cucumber and radish

It took her half an hour to choose the fish, bringing each candidate close to her face and squeezing its midsection between her fingers. As she paid, the man behind the counter admonished her for excessively handling the produce. She will not be able to go to that fishmonger again.

On the plate, the mackerel is piled in chunks next to the crisp vegetables. The presentation is awful, truly horrendous, and the fish was not suitable for the deep-frying process, but now each crispy parcel contains the danger of pain. The batter will stop the man from sliding the meat cleanly from the many small bones. He will have to pluck tenderly through every piece, or sit picking the sharp fragments from his mouth after each bite. She doesn't care which.

She no longer stands on ceremony as he begins to pick through the inconvenient dish. She crouches on the floor next to her child. She reaches out and stops herself. Instead, she says the girl's name: *Emmy. Emmy, please.*

She does not say *come to me, let me hold you, let me protect you from where this man is going to take you.* She merely opens her arms wide: come to Mummy.

The child looks up at her mother. She smiles. She does not move.

The woman reaches across her chest and unbuttons the jacket from the top. She pulls the jacket open and reveals a bra that is soaked at both nipples. She peels the triangle of material from one cup and gasps as she rips the wet breast pad from her skin. She holds herself in one hand and looks at the baby's mouth. She says *Emmy, Emmy come*.

The girl feels her mother's need and starts to crawl. Her mother coaxes her closer, closer, wiping milk from her nipple and saying the baby's name. The baby shuffles towards her mother, her mouth hanging open, her impulses still having some effect, but she stops. She looks at her mother, looks at her breast, mottled red and puffy, then tilts her head.

Emmy. Emmy, please.

The baby turns around and crawls away from her mother, towards the table, closer to the man she belongs to now.

Her mother buttons the jacket up again, wraps both forearms across her chest and squeezes herself until the pain is almost too much to bear.

entrée:
roast duck with cherries and ginger

She doesn't bother slicing the bird, serving it whole, with a handful of the gingered fruits thrown on the side. The plate clatters from her hands as she serves. Jus tips onto the placemat and she dabs at it with a napkin. She mumbles a sorry, but doesn't notice when he raises his hand to refuse the apology, as she is already on her knees, crawling towards the baby girl.

She grabs at the figure. She holds onto nothing. She says the girl's name over and over again: *Emmy, Emmy, Emmy.* The girl sits behind the man, watching his back, not taking her eyes off the man, and her mother can do nothing but plead.

He takes forever to eat the dish, and the whole time, she tries.

remove:
chestnut and wild mushroom risotto with Taleggio

She plops a ladleful of the rubbery rice into a bowl; it slops over the sides. She tosses it in front of him and he makes no attempt to excuse her serving style.

He is struggling now, and leaving longer between bites. The dish is claggy, and each forkful sticks to the roof of his mouth, making his tongue work to free the food and let him swallow. It is no good to her. The child is looking up at her chaperone, her new protector. The child is ready to go. The woman weeps.

sweet:
summer berry and mascarpone tart

The tart, of course, is too easy to consume. If she could make it again, she'd have filled it with glass.

dessert:
pears poached in sloe gin with vanilla

She sits opposite him and pushes the bowl across to his place; it slides awkwardly, spilling the crimson gin reduction all over the white cloth. She slams the liquor bottle onto the table and reaches over to take his wine glass from where it sits. She gulps down the remaining Barolo and pours the burgundy spirit almost to the rim.

She is breathing hard and staring his way. He slices so fucking calmly, dips the fruit on his fork into its liquid, lifts the morsel to the end of his face. His lips peel back from his teeth and he sets the sweet pear onto his tongue. She wishes she had bolted the door instead of setting the table.

after dinner:
coffee and a truffle

She slams the slate platter down in front of him, breaking off a corner and tipping over the chocolate cubes, but cannot let go of the edges of it. Her fists won't ungrip. She starts to keen, not quietly, but hysterically, with abandon. He pushes his chair away from the table and lets her fall into his lap, her legs touching and to the side, a child herself now. He holds her, never moving his head, barely touching, a mother for a moment. She stops heaving, stops making those sounds, but makes no attempt to move. He reaches past her to take a truffle with his fingertips and, very slowly, politely, puts out his tongue and places the truffle on it. There are three truffles on the platter. When the three are gone, she knows she has to get up.

He swallows the third. She gets up.

to finish:
a goodbye, no tip

He finishes his meal and dabs his napkin at the corners of his mouth. There is no bill to pay, no debt to settle, so he stands up slowly and puts his hand to his stomach, turning towards the woman and bending slightly at the waist. The woman makes no response. She has little to say.

The watercolour girl at the floor watches the man with no eyes, willing him to come to her, opening her arms up to his embrace. He leans down towards the child and lifts her upwards, tucking her small body into the crook of his arm. As they leave, the man turns, as if to glance once more at the mother behind him, but there are no eyes, there is no baby, there is no one to see.

I AM YOUR WRASSE

Bluestreak cleaner wrasse (*Labroides dimidiatus*)
Known for its cleaning habits, picking at and removing
ectoparasites and assorted detritus on various species of
fishes. Stereotyped signals between the two fishes help
ensure that the cleaning goes smoothly and that the cleaner
does not end up as the client's dinner.

Hogfish (*Lachnolaimus maximus*)
Sex reversal is common. All fishes begin life as females,
which can develop into males. No parental care is
given to the pelagic eggs.

– *Grzimek's Animal Life Encyclopedia,
2nd ed., Volume 5, Fishes II*

A nameless child is born to a nameless woman beneath
a bridge in a town on the outskirts of Cardiff. A grim
scene; the woman squats in shadow, dirty nails against stone.
There are people all around to hear her screams, but they all
think she's doing the things that they disprove of, snapping

a needle off under her skin or getting attacked by a client, and so they don't even turn their heads – they keep walking. Just to clarify, this is now. They could be me or you. The baby slips out easily and lands with a bump in the wet. The mother falls backwards, hitting her head on the wall, but it's not the concussion that eventually kills her, it's the slow, ruptured bleed from her insides, a death that's been long brewing. The baby's puckered mouth searches for a warm nipple but all it finds is the floor, so it attaches to what it can and sucks and swallows, and its first meal is soil and dirt and crumbs of stale tobacco. Don't worry about that baby. It survives.

No school, no family, no help. The child learns to swim by falling into the slick-brown canal and needing to get out. It learns to read from the papers covered in chip grease that are thrown to the wind. It runs its face along the floor and gently lips the matter there into its mouth. This is what sustains it.

The child grows, somehow, though not as much as the other kids do, those in houses, beneath roofs, eating from plates and sleeping in beds. Let's look in one of those houses for a moment: there, scratching, is a girl, a girl who can't remember her own name for it is used so infrequently, for she is spoken to so infrequently. Her mother did not want her. She does not unpack when she enters a new house, as she knows they, too, will not want her. She paws at her neck with her nails and flakes of skin fly; a stress-induced condition, they say, but she doesn't have files that go back longer than a few months, so would they know for sure? We won't look at her again for a little while, but keep her in your mind as she tries to find where she fits in the world, tries to find a home.

Under the bridge our child slips into the water easily, so easily it might have grown gills. It barely swims, but moves along the wall with its lips, snipping off little bites of the moss and dirt on the wall, the stuff it has learned to live on. This is not a particularly nutritional diet, and this child has grown a little strangely because of it; its lower jaw juts out so its bottom set of teeth cover the top set when its mouth is closed, and its skin has a greenish-orange pallor, but it is thriving in its own way, and clever, too. The fish in the water are healthier after its visits, having had their parasites nibbled from them, and they swim in greater numbers than before its arrival. The river water runs clearer.

One day, a large bream with a rudder injury floats into view, causing the smaller fish to panic and scatter. The child, nestling against the warm stone, approaches the bream, lying sideways, its wide eyes darting. The child gently nudges the bream with its nose, then gets to work on the dead tissue around the injury. With the scales removed and the necrosis halted, the healing can begin. The bream offers more of itself; the child feeds. The bream will recover and swim away; the child is sated. The child gets out of the water and nestles in the shadows, out of the view of everyone. Inside its body, hormones begin their work.

Skip forward, then, to a few years later. By now, our shadow-child, gangly and half-lumbering, is almost an adult, and knows the hiding places near to the bridge when the singles or couples or groups come to congregate and to do whatever they do to themselves that makes them pass out and drool. For the few hours they are there, the child takes to the park nearby, lingering in the shelter of trees, waiting to get home. Except it is beneath the bridge one night when the police come, with their extra-bright torches and their legalese, and tell the child to get out of there, to go home, to find somewhere else to sleep, to never come back. They chase the child away and then there is nothing. There is nowhere to go. There is no water, there are no walls. The park is too big, too expansive, there is nothing to press against or feed off. The child runs.

What of our girl? Since we last looked her way she has been moved around yet more, passed from loving grasp to loving grasp, then thrown away each time. She has fallen between the cracks and been pulled out, scuffed on the sides and with wounds from the falling. She has been shaken, unsettled, tossed around and the very boundaries of her body are inse-cure now, her flesh responding to trauma in ways it should not, her skin crying out and shedding itself. She wraps her body up so others might not see its condition.

She's in a home for now, but it's temporary, as they all are. She is amongst people, because they are the ones that will have her, but she knows they care little about whether she stays or goes. She's out tonight, as she is most nights, finding trouble, looking for somewhere to fit.

A left turn, a right; it is after midnight that the child rounds the corner into an alleyway and presses its face to the wall, sucking up whatever clings to it, feeding itself. Into a corner it rushes as a group of young people run into the alley, out of breath and laughing the sort of tense laughter that only comes from running from authority; relief and exhilaration and exhaustion all rolled into a cackle. They bend over and cling to their knees, filling their lungs, letting sweat drip onto the floor. One of these people is the scratching girl; you'll recognise her there, on the fringe of the group, giggling nervously, scarf around her face, staying close to the other bodies, but not too close. She always has to judge how close is okay, how far is too far. The others stop laughing and so does she.

Full of adrenaline, the male bodies push the female bodies against the wall. The girl does not like this; she pushes back, automatically, and she is thrown to the ground. They bray at her, taunt her, call her names. A siren sounds close by; they all run away and leave her there, palms in a puddle, knees bleeding. The siren screeches past, the lights illuminating the girl for just a moment, dirty water on her face, cheeks scratched from the abrasion of brick. She wipes her face and leaves a red smear. Thinking she is alone, she sits back in the puddle, pulls her scarf from her neck and scratches, a small harm to feel better. There is a movement; she looks up and sees the shadow-child.

Our nameless child, here, is seen for the first time. A person, not a thing. He finds that he is a boy, underneath someone else's gaze. With his gangly limbs and broad shoulders and slim hips and pink lips and green-tinted skin, he defies easy categorisation, but he feels it; he is a boy. He raises his jutting jaw and wriggles under the gaze of the girl.

She begins to cry, knowing loneliness and fear, and the boy goes to her. There is no language there, because why would he be able to speak? No one has ever asked him to do so. But he sees, animal reactions, that the girl is in need: food, shelter, space. She has tired flesh, and things on her skin, and wounds that need cleaning. There is a strange arrangement of a bond between them, chest to chest. She feels it too, the alien sensation of being desired. He runs a rough tongue from the corner of her mouth to the place where her tears come from, indulging in familiar salt. He lifts his fingers and inhales the blood and dirt and drinks the brown puddle water from her palms. She looks down at clean hands. She offers up her neck and he places his mouth there, uses his lips to skim the bits of black matter from her, breathes them in. He takes flakes of skin into his mouth and lets them dissolve. He reaches a cut and nibbles around the edge, taking the slight infection inside, leaving the good scabs and swallowing the rest. He takes the muck from behind her ears and leaves clean flesh behind. He restores her. She feeds him. He is nourished. She is renewed.

The boy takes his time with his tender work. The girl lets him. Beneath the flakes of skin and dirt she finds there is new skin – male skin. She finds that she has become a boy.

Around them the setting dissolves; time fractures; this is it, now, this is everywhere. They are both people, not things. Not problems. One boy has no words and the other does not speak his, but still they communicate. One says be my home, let me live in you, take me under your roof and keep me there. One says let me live on your filth, let me subsist on the flakes of your skin, let me drink the many fluids that drip from you. As the cleaner-child licks the fragments of food from between the new boy's teeth, as he sucks the sleep from his eyes, as he nibbles the bits of dried wax from the caverns of his ears, they find fresh ecstasy.

They will find a space of their own, under a bridge, in a puddle, a roof of sorts over their heads, and they will slip into the water and feed off each other.

eighth: happy endings

where there may be a saviour, of a sort, or a revelatory moment, or a gratifying conclusion, for readers need them, I am told, if they are to cope with the state of the world, and put the book down and go about their days in a manner that makes them amenable, to buy their bread so they have energy for work and to mend their clothes that are suitable for work, and to keep their heads down and believe that things will get better if they just carry on, if they don't think too much or make a fuss, and have faith in those people who style themselves as saviours, or who tell them to trust in the system as it is, just keep going, keep going, don't look at those around you, don't count yourself among the millions of others, don't look at the very seams of your body and watch it come apart, don't blur the boundaries of you and the person you hold in your arms, don't become one from two, don't become one from several, don't free yourself from the individuality that holds you alone, don't embrace a collective existence as air or as honey or as the concept of empathy, don't hold your hand out with a slice of bread for another to eat, shove all of your bread into your mouth because one day there might be none for you, either, and it is better for you not to question why that is, because otherwise you might find yourself in all sorts of trouble, making all sorts of trouble, shifting the very foundations of the world in which we all have to live. no; it is written; you cannot leave the book upset. so have your happy endings, such as they are

THIS IS MY BODY, GIVEN FOR YOU

Fermentation

No visitors, no letters, no laughing nor playing. They were children no longer; they were servants of God. They lived in cement cells with thin mattresses on the beds and cold water in the pipes. They had bible teachings all morning and work in the afternoon. They were looked after by twelve priests, all sour-faced and all with little patience for the young.

Self-sufficiency was key. The girls had to learn to look after themselves and others, so they milled flour from locally harvested wheat, churned cheese from local cows, made juice from the apples in their own orchard. They baked the thin wafers of the Body of Christ that they took in their mouths every morning at Mass as they knelt gingerly, their knees sore from crawling across stone, punishments given to make the girls learn the errors of their ways. The priests did not agree with spending money – not when the devil was waiting to make work for idle hands.

Lily, the new girl, was placed in the library, where her job was to neaten and tidy, to stack and arrange, to sit in a room alone and not cause any trouble. On the shelves there were only books that taught the girls what they needed to know: how to grow food, how to feed others, how good women should behave. Lily made it her mission to devour every issue of the *Farmer's Almanac*.

Lily had grown up with a baker mother and a farmer father. Her brother had learned to brew cider to support the family, and as a child she'd watched as each one perfected their craft. She spent her new hours with the almanacs filling the gaps in her knowledge, and soon she started visiting the kitchen after her library hours were over, teaching the other girls how to bake and brew and churn with skill, their knuckles rapped to bruises. They told each other how they'd arrived there; what sin they had committed to be sent away from home. They laughed and threw flour and were children once more, a brief respite from the rest of their existence.

As the girls in the kitchen improved under Lily's tutelage, the priests commented that the bread was lighter and airier, that the cheese was smoother and more tart. Lily suggested that Mass would be more enjoyable if the Host was her own sourdough, sliced thinly to mimic the wafers. After tasting her toast, the priests agreed. Lily, gambling on better treatment for herself and for the others if she pandered to the men, told the priests that she could make something else too, something that would ease the stress of their dutiful lives. They brought her an apple press and yeast and bottles, and they moved her responsibilities from the library to the kitchen.

Lily showed the girls how to make cider in barrels; forty litres at a time. She took the seeds from the apple pulp, washed them and saved them, every single one, promising herself and the others that when the time came, when they were released, they would use them to plant their very own orchard, so that they could make money and look after themselves. The cider was sweet and tangy and very alcoholic. The priests took to drinking in the evenings, and it turned their cruelty in a new direction. They stumbled in the darkness, all hands and shushing lips.

It started with just one of the priests, and it started with Lily. He took her in the nights, when the others could hear.

Life went on as it had. Lily still made the bread and churned the cheese and brewed the cider.

In the kitchen the next day, her mind turning, she took handfuls of apples from the cider pile and chewed them until she could chew them no more. She spat the matter into a metal jug and took another mouthful. She chewed and spat until her jaw ached. She juiced the pulp, covered it with a tea towel, set it aside from the rest of the cider, and went to bed to await her visitors.

By morning the process had already started. She added a little yeast and she went back day after day, but she waited. Her saliva sped up the process; after two weeks the special cider was ready. She could smell the alcoholic sweetness, could see the fermentation bubbles. She served it to the priests that night. They gulped it rather than sipped. It made them drunker than usual, and they came at her, this time in numbers.

But as they took her in the darkness, she thought: I am inside you.

Leaven

Lily grew sick, and then sore, and then larger by the day. She recognised the signs and said nothing. Her formless smocks covered her growing midriff, but as their hands slipped around her waist and onto her stomach at night, each one of them felt it. Each one broke a cold sweat and stopped, mumbling about the sanctity of human life and the indignity of fornication while pregnant. Each one, after a moment, continued.

She was not permitted to stop working. She kneaded the bread and churned the butter. She made the cider. The other girls helped as much as they could, but were shooed away by the priests and were beaten for trying. Lily passed eight months and could barely carry herself around the building, but if they saw her idle, they beat her.

While stirring the milk, Lily noticed wet patches on her chest. Her nipples, preparing for the child, were premature in their expulsion of milk. Alone in the kitchen, she lifted her shirt and gently pressed her breasts; thin streams of watery-white liquid ran from both nipples, more freely than she'd imagined they could. She squeezed herself until no more would run, and she smiled as it dripped into the curdling milk in the pail. She stirred to combine, watching it disappear into the mixture, and when she served the soft cheese up to the twelve priests, she had to turn away to keep from grinning. She was inside them.

The rise

She squeezed and screamed and sweated out the baby in a bathroom on her own. None of the others were allowed inside, and the priests locked the door until the commotion was over. They gave her blankets and towels for it, but refused further mention. The baby was a boy and she called it Grace.

It was three days until the priests started coming again. Her wet breasts, her ripe hips, the blood that would trickle from her after the act; they loved it all. Only when she grew sore and red, with white discharge leaking out and onto her underwear, did they change their methods. They spat in disgust and took her in her other orifices, where there was more pain but less trouble for them.

She was expected to work from a week after the birth, once she could settle the child and keep it quiet. The other girls crept into the kitchen to hold Grace when they could, and when none could come, Lily sat him on the counter, on the wheat sacks, on the cold floor, on her feet. She sifted and she churned and she brewed. Still her body grew more painful. She stopped drinking water because going to the toilet hurt so much her teeth tore into her cheeks. The mess in her underwear grew thicker and more yellow. Still the priests did not permit her to stop.

The solution came to her at night on a Friday, after their visits, when she lay awake both numb and alive with rage, the baby fastened to her breast, her hand stuck into her underwear to try and relieve the pain. She heard the screech of violation from another room – the first time it had been anyone but her. She removed her fingers from inside herself and brought them up to shift the baby; she caught the sweet-sour, bready scent from beneath her nails, from the whiteish mess, and a voice spoke. She thought of the kitchen, of the oven. She lulled herself to sleep with the comforting thought of it, and the next morning she woke up feeling rested and alive.

She caught the other girls at their jobs, noting the dark circles around some of their eyes, the heaviness of their steps, and asked them to go and fetch her some apples from the orchard. She took the baby to the kitchen and took the bread starter from its place on the shelf. She took a scoop of it and transferred it to a new bowl. With a chair against the door, she slipped down her underwear and slid three fingers inside herself, the pain almost dropping her to the floor. When she drew them out, they were yellow-white. She took a wooden spoon and scraped the discharge into the starter, to which she added a little more flour and a little more water. She pulled up her underwear and left the mixture aside to grow. This part would bring her a bitter pleasure, but it would not do what she needed it to do.

The girls brought her apples, as many as she'd asked for. She thanked them, kissing their cheeks, before sending them out of the kitchen, away from any blame. She peeled the apples, dicing them into small cubes, and set them on the stove in a thick pan with as much sugar as there was fruit. Setting the chair against the kitchen door once more, she retrieved her apple seeds from their hiding place at the back of a dark cupboard at the far end of the room. By that time, there were three glass jars full of them – hundreds, perhaps thousands of the things. The girls had been saving them too. She had no time to count them, or to work out whether they'd be enough.

She put a jarful of the seeds into a hessian bag and smashed them to pieces with a rolling pin. Her arm strained with the weight, but she kept going, kept going, until the seeds were no more, and in their place was a pile of rough, crushed, toxic apple-seed powder. Into the pan they went, stirred to combine, thickening the jam so much that she could barely move the spoon. She turned the heat off and poured it into jars; it was golden orange with thousands of flecks of red, almost more seed than apple.

The bread starter was bubbling and full of air. She made a dough, folded it in, and left it overnight to rise.

By Sunday morning, it was brimming over the edges of the loaf pan, more active than she'd ever seen it before. She pushed it into the oven and spent the next twenty-five minutes feeding her baby, their baby, the one they'd all created.

She cooled it and halved it and sliced it into thin, tongue-sized segments, crispy and tasty and perfect for a ceremony. She took twelve slices and placed them at the front of the communion tray, saving the rest for later. She delivered it to the priest in the usual manner, on the usual platter, and though it was thicker and differently shaped to their usual offerings, the smell of the freshly baked body was too much to refuse. As each of the twelve clergymen took their turns to kneel, they opened their mouths wide and the priest placed the bread from the front of the tray on their tongues. They each held it there, ecstatically savouring, letting the lord himself melt into their mouths and seep into their systems, and she felt an excitement that tingled through her, that almost made her laugh. She served the rest of the bread to them later, loaded with the apple jam, topped with the soft cheese, with a glass of the fermented drink. They drank and she fed them more and more, until the jam jars were almost empty. They were full and delirious when they went to bed. A special evening treat.

Lily lay in bed, clutching Grace, waiting for the hour when the first of them would usually arrive. None came. She stared up at the ceiling until daybreak, then walked slowly, calmly, to the priests' quarters. She pushed open the door of the first bedroom. He was there, on his knees, pools of his own watery shit around him, blood streaming from his mouth and crotch, his hands clutching at his stomach and throat. Yellow-white discharge at the corners of his mouth. Shouting out the name of God, deliriously quoting verse, reality far from his finger. She checked all twelve rooms and they were all the same: white spots in the mouth, cracked lips, dry, split tongue, vicious incontinence, haemorrhaging from all orifices, screaming for their lives.

The noise brought down the rest of the girls. They stood, hands at their mouths, trembling, hardly daring to see what they were seeing, hardly believing. Lily pointed at the flecks of seed in the streams of vomit; she showed the girls the white mess at the men's mouths. Gripping her swaddled child, Lily pulled up her dress and pushed her fingers inside herself again, to show them: a filth-fingered liberator with a baby in her arms.

CHOOSE YOUR OWN

read in the order given

or

start at number 1, and choose path A

or

start at number 1, and choose path B

1. You place a plate of bacon and eggs by the side of the bed. Your wife's eyes are open, but she does not acknowledge you. You kiss her on the forehead. You open the curtains to let in the light. She does not move. You kiss her again.

As you head out of the front door, you glance backwards. You see that the curtains are closed once more.

Go to number 2.

2. You talk to your wife about babies. She does not respond. You mention her age and dwindling egg production; you produce a pamphlet her mother sent, on the dangers of late pregnancy. She lolls her head to the window, her lips slightly parted. You say

163

that you'd like to have at least two. She lets out a long, bovine moan.

Choose.

Path A. Go to number 13.

Path B. Go to number 10.

3. Your wife watches television. Tears stream from her eyes onto her swollen belly. You wipe her expressionless face with a tissue, mop the puddle on her dress, plant a kiss on her large stomach. Sitting beside her, you put your arm around her shoulders, tilt her head so it rests on your chest, and change the channel.

Choose.

Path A. Go to number 5.

Path B. Go to number 6.

4. You search for an old medical textbook. You find it under the sofa. You open it, turn it to the page you remember.

The patient's surgically induced childhood can pose a challenge for caregivers. In this case a system of rewards (ice-cream) and punishments (smacks) allows for the patient to be trained back into manageable behaviour.

You close the book. Open it again. Fold the corner of the page and leave it on the coffee table.

Choose.

Path A. Go to number 9.

Path B. Go to number 7.

5. Your wife appears in the kitchen, trousers on back to front. You stand in front of her, pointing at her legs. You say *Look. What's wrong?* You repeat this over and over. Finally, she shuffles to the bedroom. She returns fixed. You scoop strawberry ice-cream from a large tub in the freezer, top it with sprinkles, and give it to her. She smiles.

Choose.
Path A. Go to number 15.
Path B. Go to number 8.

6. You wake at 3 a.m., full of frustration. You kiss your wife. She opens her eyes, glassy in the dark. Her mouth does not respond to yours. Her tongue lies heavy and passive. You stroke sweat-drenched hair from her temple. Heft her into a sitting position. You pull her ratty T-shirt over her head. Take her full breast in your hand, then your mouth. You suck, lick, kiss. She does not respond. Does not attempt to stop you. You move down between her legs, find her wet, are encouraged. With your tongue inside her, you look up and see her cow eyes staring at the wall. You burst into tears. Lay her down and turn her onto her side. You masturbate in the bathroom, crying.

Choose.
Path A. Go to number 8.
Path B. Go to number 15.

165

7.　You walk to the kitchen for breakfast. Your wife is there, dangling a knife into the toaster. The toaster is on. She electrocutes herself, screeches, falls back to the floor. You go to her, cradle her head, quiet her vacant wailing. You say *See?*

Choose.

Path A. Go to number 4.

Path B. Go to number 9.

8.　You climb into the loft and retrieve the machine. It is still stained. You place it onto the kitchen table. You reach out, touch the protruding instruments, try to wiggle them. Still sharp, still glued firmly in place. You place your head under the halo. You vomit into your hands.

Choose.

Path A. Go to number 11.

Path B. Go to number 3.

9.　You show your wife how to put the teabag into the cup. How to wait for the kettle to boil. How to pour in the water, stir it, remove the teabag. How to pour in the milk. She tries, spills, you slap her face. She tries, forgets the teabag, you slap her again. Her face reddening, she tries, she finally gets it right. You present her with a bowl of strawberry ice-cream with sprinkles on top. You remember from a dusty textbook: *as biddable as cattle.*

Choose.
Path A. Go to number 6.
Path B. Go to number 5.

10. You find a note from your wife. Her handwriting is unusual. The note reads: 'Do try to love me still'.
Choose.
Path A. Go to number 14.
Path B. Go to number 11.

11. You wake at 3 a.m., full of frustration. You kiss your wife. She opens her eyes, glassy in the black. Her mouth does not respond to yours. You roll her onto her side, slip your hands inside her T-shirt, enter her from behind. You thrust your hips against her. She emits a ceaseless lowing. You finish, wipe her thighs dry with a tissue, kiss her shoulder and say *Sorry.* She does not move. You sleep soundly.
Choose.
Path A. Go to number 12.
Path B. Go to number 13.

12. The screen shows the outline of your child, tethered. Your throat closes and you weep. Your wife displays no reaction. You say *Look.* Your wife looks at the screen. Says nothing. The nurses glance at each other, go out of the room. You see them speaking to each other through the window. You will do without the rest of the scans.

Choose.
Path A. Go to number 3.
Path B. Go to number 4.

13. You bring home a takeaway. You call your wife's
name. Engineering journals and dusty medical
textbooks are scattered across the living room floor.
You start to tidy them. You notice the title of the
one on top:

> *Psychosurgery: Intelligence, emotion and social
> behaviour following prefrontal lobotomy for mental
> disorders. Dr Walter Freeman.*

It slips from your fingers and lands open. You read.

> *The personality of the patient was changed in some
> way in the hope of rendering him more amenable to
> the social pressures under which he is supposed to exist.*

You call your wife's name again. And again.

Choose.
Path A. Go to number 10.
Path B. Go to number 14.

14. You find your wife sitting at the kitchen table, her
face pressed into a machine. A metal halo, padded
with leather, tilts her head to one side, then the
other. Slowly, methodically. Blood streams from her
eyes. You faint. You come around. There is a syringe
in her arm, spent. Her upper eyelids are pulled back
by hooks. Two tiny medical spears stab her through
the eye sockets, above her eyes, embedded in her

brain, severing connections as the halo moves her head. The machine stops. Her back rises and falls with gentle breath. She hums a light, unconscious note.

Choose.

Path A. Go to number 7.

Path B. Go to number 12.

15. Your wife watches television. Beside her are knitting needles, still cast on to an unfinished project. You placed them there. You watch her for a moment. You turn back to your book.

Choose.

Path A. Go to number 16.

Path B. Go to number 16.

16. You marvel at the machine your wife built. Neat, precise, inspired. You flick the switch on the side and watch it spring to life. It works as you imagine it would. You flick the switch again, and the machine resets.

You pull out the kitchen chair. Sit yourself down. You look over at your wife. She does not see you. You wipe your face dry, calm your breath, settle your head into the leather-covered halo. You count down from three and flick the switch.

No need to choose again.

PUBLICATIONS HISTORY

Amelia Magdalene was first published in the Fear and Fantasy issue of *The Stinging Fly* (winter 2016)

The Bastard-Octopus was first published in *Gutter 18* (autumn 2018)

The Small Island was first published in *F(r)iction No 11* (2018) and *The Best of British Fantasy 2018*

Mr Fox was first published in *We Were Always Here: A Queer Words Anthology* (2019)

The Professional was first published in *Mslexia Issue 81* (2019)

'Til Death Do Us Parts was first published on the 3 of Cups Patreon (2020)

Coo was first published in *Grain 47.2* (winter 2020)

Wet Like Jelly was first published in *New Writing Scotland 35* (2017)

Human Mummy Confection was first published in *Gutter 20* (2020)

This Is My Body, Given For You was first published in *New Gothic Review Volume 2* (2020)

Choose Your Own was first published in *Mycelia Issue 2* (summer 2019)

The Bastard-Octopus is a response to the Roland Barthes book *Mythologies*, specifically the essay 'The World of Wrestling' and the line '[T]he most repugnant bastard there is: the bastard–octopus'.

ACKNOWLEDGEMENTS

Enormous thanks to:

Kirsty Logan, Camilla Grudova and Heather Palmer for being the voices I trust the most with my work, and for making me change the titles of my books when they're shit;

Jennie Creitzman, Laurence de Clippele, Elly Gilbert, Charley Tassaker, Hayley Cox, Gemma Milne, Julia Armfield, Alice Slater, Esther Clayton, Nyla Ahmad, Katie Goh and Anna Walsh for the beautiful friendship and endless support;

Brandy Anderson for the conversation about death on a Hong Kong beach that led to *A Meal for the Man in Tails;*

my agent, Emma Shercliff, who loved these weird stories first and foremost;

my publisher Rebecca Wojturska, who is just one of many incredible people running small and brave indie presses (or magazines) in an increasingly hostile landscape; these indies are vital and deserve more support;

every publisher, editor, magazine and awards scheme that ushered these stories along, and especially Mia Gallagher, who first paid me for a short story and edited *Amelia Magdelene* with generosity and grace;

my families;

D.

THE CREDITS

Creating a book takes a massive team effort. Haunt and Heather Parry would like to thank everyone who worked behind the scenes on *This Is My Body, Given For You*.

Managing Director and Editor
Rebecca Wojturska

Copy-editor
Ross Stewart

Proofreader
Kirstyn Smith

Cover Designer
Esther Clayton

Typesetter
Laura Jones

Contracts Consultant
Caro Clarke

ABOUT THE AUTHOR

Heather Parry is a fiction writer and editor originally from Rotherham, South Yorkshire. She is the co-founder and Editorial Director of *Extra Teeth* magazine, co-host of the *Teenage Scream* podcast and the Scottish Senior Policy & Liaison Manager for the Society of Authors, a trade union for writers. In 2021 she created the free-access *Illustrated Freelancer's Guide* with artist Maria Stoian.

She won the 2016 Bridge Award for an Emerging Writer, Cove Park's 2017 Emerging Writer residency, the Laxfield Literary Launch Prize in 2021 and was a Hawthornden Fellow in 2021. Her short stories and nonfiction have been published internationally and her debut novel, *Orpheus Builds a Girl*, was released in October 2022 by Gallic Books.

Heather lives in Glasgow with her partner and their cats, Ernesto and Fidel.